Finding Love

Toni Shiloh

Finding Love by Toni Shiloh
© 2017 by Celebrate Lit Publishing. All rights reserved.

First Edition June, 2017

ISBN 13: 978-0999145104
ISBN 10: 099914510X

No part of this book may be reproduced in any written, electronic, recording, or photocopying form without written permission of the publisher, Celebrate Lit Publishing.

Books may be purchased by contacting the publisher,
Celebrate Lit Publishing
 29078 Whitegate Lane
Highland, CA, 92346
or by email at celebratelit@gmail.com.

Published by: Celebrate Lit Publishing
Cover Design by: Chautona Havig
Commissioning Editor: Denise Barela, Celebrate Lit Publishing
10 9 8 7 6 5 4 3 2 1

Praise for Finding Love

"This second visit to the quaint community of Maple Run is even better than the first! Mouthwatering food, a swoon-inducing hero (complete with dimples and military uniform), adorable children, and a compelling heroine (complete with a great family and a yummy restaurant) - just one of those elements would be reason enough to love Finding Love. All of them together, plus a tender story of second chances and trusting God? Yes please!"

~ Carrie Schmidt, Reading Is My SuperPower

"Toni Shiloh's Finding Love is a sweet tale of overcoming fears to find not just love, but trust in the Lord. She weaves a powerful tale amid some beautiful romance and a few giggles, bringing a satisfied, swoony-sigh at its conclusion. I already want to revisit Maple Run to catch up with its sweet residents!"

~ Mikal Dawn, author of Count Me In

Dedication

To the Author and Finisher of my faith.

Acknowledgements

To Sandra Barela: Sandy, I can't thank you enough for the love and effort you put into my books. You're more than a publisher, you're a friend. Thank you for everything from the bottom of my heart!

To the Celebrate Lit team: I appreciate the dedication and talent of the editors and cover designer. Thank you for making sure *Finding Love* shines inside and out. Blessings to all of you!

To my husband: Thank you for encouraging me. For telling others about my books and just for simply loving me.

To my boys: I love you. Never forget to love everyone.

To Melissa Henderson, Kara Esselbach, and Tanya Saldana: Thank you so much for offering me feedback on how to make this story better. Y'all encouraged me and helped me find those nuances I would have missed. I appreciate the time you took to read *Finding Love* and offer me feedback. Sending prayers and blessings your way.

To Ronie Kendig: Thank you for your friendship and mentorship. I appreciate you taking the time to help me tighten up my writing and looking for weak spots. No matter how busy you are, you always have a time to offer encouragement. You're always in my prayers, friend!

To the readers: Thank you so much for taking a trip to Maple Run with me. I pray you enjoy the tale.

Chapter One

Luke Robinson rolled into The Maple Pit's parking lot. The restaurant looked like a refurbished barn; its red siding gleamed in the summer sunshine. He'd driven to Maple Run, Virginia, for one purpose.

But right then his stomach demanded sustenance, curtailing his plans. He turned off the Harley Roadster and placed his boot-clad feet on the ground. Hopefully, one of the staff members could direct him to his real purpose…after they fed him.

Rising, he stretched, allowing his spine to decompress, and took his off helmet. The summer breeze blew across his face, cooling the sweat that clung to his nape and the back of his ears.

The cool air was a welcomed relief after having his face stuck in a "brain bucket" for the past few hours. His stomach grumbled; its demands louder than before. In a few steps he strode into the restaurant.

A pretty redhead greeted him. "Welcome to The Maple Pit." Her eyes widened as she took in his appearance.

Was it his six-foot-three frame, leather apparel, or scruffy face that did her in? Since his boots had hit American soil, he'd been growing out the hair on his face.

Judging by the relaxing ambiance and dress of their customers, he'd bank on his appearance being the reason for the look of astonishment on the hostess' face.

"Thank you, ma'am." His voice sounded a little rusty as thirst pushed against his throat.

"Would you like to sit at the bar?"

Luke glanced around. Families were enjoying their meals in booths and tables. Was there really a point in taking up a table for just himself? He glanced at the bar. A tightness in his gut brought forth beads of sweat.

"Um, sure."

"Great, this way."

She headed toward his right, a menu in hand. After placing it on the countertop, she smiled at him. "Your server will be right with you."

He nodded, then straddled the stool and picked up the menu. *Oh, man.* The food reminded him of his grandmother's cooking. In his opinion, Rosa Robinson was the best cook in west Texas.

A small smile tugged at his lips as he thought about the petite woman who ran the Robinson men better than any four-star general ever could. Once the Army had released him on R&R—rest and relaxation—he'd hopped on his roadster and headed straight for Virginia.

The need to make amends pressed down upon him. Now, he regretted not taking the time to see his grandmother before he left. She would have calmed him.

A mature African-American woman came out of the kitchen. A frown on her face etched deep lines across her forehead. She paused in front of him. "Excuse me, sir. Have you been helped?"

"No, ma'am."

Her frown intensified. "I'm so sorry. I'll go find your server."

"No worries. I'm in no hurry." He offered her a smile despite the objection coming from his stomach.

"Thank you for your patience." She rounded a corner and disappeared.

Was there a breakroom back there where a server was hiding out?

His gaze landed on the menu again, skimming the offerings. They served Arnold Palmers, a sweet tea and lemonade concoction. His mouth salivated imagining the taste of the drink he hadn't tasted in months. It would be the perfect way to quench his thirst.

A shadow fell across the bar distracting him from the list of entrees. He looked up into the most gorgeous brown eyes he'd ever seen.

"Delaney Jones," he whispered.

Her eyes widened, wariness coloring her gaze. "Do I know you?"

"No, ma'am. But, I knew your husband, Jones. I mean Parker Jones." His words stumbled over themselves in the face of her beauty.

"You knew Parker?"

Her warm voice flowed over him. He swallowed. "Yes, ma'am. We served together on his last tour." He licked his lips. "Sorry for your loss, ma'am." *Was three years too late to give his condolences?*

"Thank you." She cocked her head to the side. "That's a lot of ma'ams. I doubt I'm older than you."

"True, but when you've been adding 'ma'am' and 'sir' for almost twenty years…" He shrugged. "It becomes ingrained."

"You can call me by my name."

"Thank you, Mrs. Jones."

She shook her head. "How about you call me Delaney?"

He'd said her name over and over on the ride up here. Somehow saying her first name aloud seemed disrespectful to Jones's memory. Yet, she stood there waiting expectantly. "Delaney."

"Thank you, Mister…"

"Oh, Luke Robinson." He half rose as he offered a hand in greeting.

She slid her hand in his and attraction rushed up his arm faster than a lightning bolt. *Whoa.*

Her face flushed.

Did she feel the same thing?

"Nice to meet you, Mr. Robinson."

"*Mr.* Robinson is at home, sitting in a recliner. Probably reading a newspaper. You can call me Robinson."

She tugged at her hand.

Embarrassment heated his face as he realized he still held hers. He dropped it, wondering at the warmth left by her touch.

"I can't call you Robinson."

"Well, the guys call me that or Crusoe."

A grin graced her full pink lips. "I'll call you Luke if you call me Delaney."

She's Jones's wife. Don't forget, Robinson.

"So, did you come here to eat or to see me?" Her voice trailed as her face flushed.

Finding Love 5

"Two birds. Just didn't realize The Maple Pit would be the stone."

A brief look of confusion crossed her face, then she nodded as if the use of his broken cliché clicked in her understanding. "Then what can I get you to eat?"

"I'm kind of hungry." *That was an understatement.* He ran a hand over his chin. "What do you recommend?"

"The create-your-own platter. You could get a main dish and two sides." She pointed to the menu. "Maybe maple fried chicken or the maple meatloaf."

His eyebrows crept toward his hairline. "Maple meatloaf?"

"We use maple bacon and put a touch of maple in the sauce."

Meatloaf and bacon? What could be better? "Sounds perfect."

"What sides?"

"Uh..." He glanced back down at the menu. "Garlic mashed potatoes and the collard greens." His stomach grumbled in anticipation.

"Drink?"

"Arnold Palmer." He couldn't have prevented the grin if he'd tried. It'd been awhile since he drank anything other than Gatorade or water.

"Coming right up."

He watched as her tall frame sauntered off toward the kitchen. She had to be close to six feet, and she carried it well. No slouching to hide her height, and there was no denying her gracefulness or femininity.

Delaney Jones. The attraction he felt at her touch was unexpected...and a huge problem. *Lord, you gotta help me out here. There's no way I can say what I need to say feeling like that around her.*

Then again, when he did…his words would affect them more than a bucket of ice water. Of course, that's assuming she was as attracted to him as he was to her *and* wanting to act on it. He took a deep breath.

No way could he act on it.

Not after what he'd done.

He ran a hand down his face, his guilt pressing in. Coming to Maple Run just became a lot more complicated than he'd anticipated.

Delaney stared at her notepad but couldn't make out a word she'd written on it. All she could see was the image of Luke Robinson. His black wavy hair lay tousled, with the lower part of his face covered by a beard. He looked like a mountain man.

A very *handsome* mountain man with ice blue eyes, tanned skin, and a Southern drawl that made her shiver with awareness. Never had a white man captivated her attention so swiftly.

But as fascinating as his looks were, what shocked her more was that he knew Parker.

Her eyes squeezed shut as she thought of her late husband. She saw him daily in the face of her twin boys whenever they were having fun. Their grins were pure Parker Jones.

Somehow, the rugged biker—dressed in leather and wearing a Harley Davidson jacket—knew him. Said he'd been on tour with him. How was it possible that he was in the military?

Finding Love 7

Sure, the Army didn't require high-and-tight haircuts like the Marines, but that man had way too much hair on his face and on the top of his head. *It suits him.*

She sighed. Maybe he was on leave and decided not to get a haircut. That would explain the abundance of it or maybe his hair grew fast.

"Everything okay, Delaney?" Nikki asked.

Delaney met the hostess' brown eyes, clouded with concern. It was such a contrast to her bubbly personality that all she could do was blink for a moment. "Yeah, I'm all right."

"You sure?" Her eyes sparkled. "It wouldn't have anything to do with the guy that walked in, huh?"

"Actually, sort of. He knew Parker."

Nikki's eyes widened. "Oh my, for reals? Are you okay?"

"I am." She straightened, imagining pulling herself together. "I'll be good."

It was sweet of Nikki to worry. She was thankful for the tight-knit Maple Pit family. Her mother and father had opened the restaurant after retirement, and slowly but surely, each new employee became family.

"All right."

"Thanks, Nikki."

"Sure." Nikki beamed and headed for the front.

Delaney turned in the meal ticket and then snuck a glance toward the bar. Luke's words came back to her. He'd come to see her. Why? Was it about Parker? She rolled her eyes.

Of course it was about Parker.

What else would it be about?

Her insides clenched as she watched Luke sit calmly. He wasn't fiddling with a cell phone. Sitting out in the open made her cringe and worry about what others were thinking. How could he be so calm and full of confidence? The man was an enigma.

Surprisingly, she wanted to know more.

She grabbed his drink and took a deep breath before heading his way. Whatever he had to say about Parker...well, she would just have to handle it.

"Your food will be out shortly." She sat the drink down and slid her hands into her Maple Pit apron.

"Thank you." He took a long swig and let out a satisfied sigh.

Blech. Why anyone would want to mix lemonade and sweet tea was beyond her, but it was a popular choice.

"That hit the spot. It's been a long trip."

"Where did you drive from?"

"Texas."

"What? On a bike?"

His black eyebrows rose, lines appearing across his forehead. Everything about him screamed...*man.*

It was so strange to feel attracted to a man who wasn't her husband. The first year after Parker's death had been spent in a black pit of depression. The second year she focused on the boys.

Now...now she was simply living.

Luke's deep laugh seemed to wrap her in a hug. "Yes, on a bike." He shrugged. "It's my favorite way to get from point A to B. You ride?"

Her laugh was quick. "No. Never."

"I could give you a ride sometime."

No way was she getting any closer to him than she had to...other than to serve his meal. "No, thank you."

He nodded in acceptance.

Finding Love

"What did you want to tell me?" She bit her lip. "I mean, you said you came to see me, right? About Parker?"

His cool blue eyes darkened to the color of a stormy sky. "Yes." His long fingers tapped on the bar's surface. "Could we maybe talk about it later? When you're not working?"

"Uh, yes, I guess so." *No, tell me now.* She cleared her throat. "Are you staying in town for a few days?"

"Yes." He ran a hand over his hair as if the day's travel just caught up to him. "Can you recommend a good hotel?" Weariness creased his face.

"Excuse me, Delaney," her mother interrupted. "Have you seen Dwight?"

Her twin brother, Dwight, was one of the chefs. "He was talking to Nina in the office, last I saw." Usually he cooked during the dinner crowd, but sometimes he switched to spend time with his wife, Nina.

Her mother looked at her then darted her eyes to Luke.

"Oh, Ma, this is Luke. He knew Parker."

"Did you really?" Her mother shook Luke's hand. "It's so nice to meet you. Did you serve with him?"

"Yes, ma'am."

"Thank you so much for your service, young man."

"Thank you kindly for the support."

Delaney shivered at his Texas drawl. The low tenor of his voice made her think of moonlit nights and starry skies.

"Are you staying in the area?" her mother asked, continuing with the third degree. The woman could be so nosy at times.

"Yes, I was just asking Delaney about hotels."

"Oh, I'll have no such thing," her mother retorted.

Delaney turned to her mother. She was sure her eyes had tried to jump out of their sockets. *What?!*

"You'll have to stay with us."

"Uh, Mother…" she lowered her voice. "Ma'am, I couldn't do that. I'm a stranger."

Delaney wanted to shoot a look of relief to Luke, but perhaps that was a little too rude. It's not that she didn't trust him to be who he claimed to be. She just had no way to prove it.

Plus, Dwight would flip if he thought she and her mother weren't being cautious around strangers. He was a tad paranoid, and she loved him for it.

"Oh, nonsense. Any friend of Parker's is a friend of ours. Isn't that right, Delaney?" Her mother nudged her with a hip.

Her lips parted in disbelief. Why couldn't a black hole swallow her up right now? Her gaze inadvertently drifted to Luke.

His blue eyes lit with suppressed laughter. She was sure his shoulders were trying not to shake. "As much as I appreciate the offer, ma'am, I respectfully decline. Insomnia makes me an annoying housemate."

Relief coursed through her body.

"I understand," her Ma said. "The nearest hotel is probably in Ashburn. We do have a local B&B, but I'm not sure if Bella is booked. Shall I call her for you?"

"Yes, please."

"Such good manners." Her mother grinned as she walked away.

"Sorry she put you on the spot like that." Delaney flipped her ponytail behind her shoulder, trying to regain her composure.

"That's okay. What time is your shift over? Is there someplace we could go and talk about...about your husband?" His voice deepened, laced with something that sounded an awful like caution.

Uneasiness tingled up her spine. "Um, I get off at six."

Suddenly his visit no longer seemed like a smile from God but one from the evil one. Why else would any of Parker's friends or army buddies suddenly drop out of the clear blue sky?

Lord, please don't let it be horrible.

Chapter Two

The queen-sized wrought-iron bed seemed impossibly small. Luke stared at it skeptically. Ms. Bella, the owner of Maple Run's Bed and Breakfast, insisted it was a queen.

Compared to his California King, it might as well have been the twin-sized cot he used on deployments. With a sigh, he dropped his duffel bag at the foot of the bed. Leaning over, he tugged one boot off then the other.

Finally, he laid down.

Thank You for getting me here safe and sound.

His body hummed, tension slowly trying to eke its way out, and his breathing slowed. The sound of his pulse drummed in his ears as he tried to focus on relaxing. His feet pressed against the iron bars in the footboard.

Groaning, he wiggled until his legs slid through, allowing his body to stretch out.

Inhale.

Exhale.

Nothing. His thoughts whirled, a picture of the B&B appeared in his mind. The white clapboard siding with green shuttered windows. Its wraparound porch reminded him of lazy summer days and the sweet tea Ms. Bella had offered the moment he walked through her front door. The whole place was just as quaint as the town of Maple Run. After leaving The Maple Pit, exhaustion had weighed heavily upon him. His trip from Texas had been long and arduous. He pushed himself, knowing he only had so long before his leave was up.

The Army granted him a month's leave, thanks to the abundant excess he'd accrued from a deployment or two. He promised to come back with a decision to reenlist for another two years or put in his paperwork for separation. With two years left to retirement, he'd be foolish not to re-up.

It was no wonder his body refused to relax with his mind hopping from subject to subject. *Go to sleep. Get some shut-eye.* Instead, an image of Delaney appeared.

"Gorgeous," he breathed out.

God knew what he was doing giving her those doe-shaped eyes the color of mahogany. They sucked him into their depths. Her black hair had been pulled into a ponytail at her nape, loose waves hanging free.

When he stood after paying his check, he realized he was right. She was tall, a few inches shorter than him.

The urge to pull her close and kiss her had shocked him. It'd been awhile since a woman created that type of reaction. The fact that it was Jones's widow made him feel worse than a dog with fleas. He groaned, running a hand down his face.

This was *not* good.

Being attracted to a dead soldier's wife was all kinds of wrong in his book.

Lord, what am I going to do?

It was time to remember why he came. He sat up, a renewed sense of purpose coursing through his veins. If he practiced his speech, maybe he wouldn't trip up when she turned those beautiful brown eyes his way.

Or stare overtly at her curves. He punched the mattress. "She's a widow and a mother of two." *Right?* He seemed to recall Jones talking about his boys.

Twins.

He groaned. "You have no business thinking of her as an attractive woman," he murmured to himself. "Jones's widow. Mother of twins." The litany fell from his lips.

His palms turned clammy. His mouth suddenly dry. The thought of twins…well, he and kids didn't fare so well. He was terrified of them and they knew it. Being an only child stunted him a little.

Not having a mom had increased the lack-of-friends factor. Living in a home with a father and grandmother cemented him in the weirdo section.

What does it matter? He wasn't staying in Maple Run. Wasn't here for any other purpose than to make amends. He certainly wasn't there to cozy up to Jones's widow and kids.

"You're here to help. Don't forget."

Who knew, he'd probably be leaving at first light once he appropriately apologized. If she let him get it all out. Delaney would hit the roof.

A glance at his sports watch told him that he had a couple of hours before it was time to meet up with her at the local park, a half hour after her shift was over. What was he supposed to do until then?

Sleep was apparently out of the question.

His cell phone vibrated, interrupting his line of thinking. His grandmother's face flashed on the screen. "Hey, Gram."

"Luke Robinson, where are you?"

He chuckled at the exasperation in her voice. She was probably standing with her hand on her hip, foot tapping in irritation. "Virginia."

She gasped. "You've gone to see the widow, haven't ya?"

"Yes, ma'am. Needed to."

"I know you think you do." A paused followed. "Have you told her?"

"No, ma'am."

"Hmm, I'll be praying for ya. You be sure to call me, so I can tell you I told you so."

Luke shook his head. His grandmother insisted he had nothing to atone for, but he knew better. "I'll call you."

"Humph. You better. Your father is driving me crazy. You need to finish your business and hurry home before I beat him with my rolling pin."

He laughed, a lightness filtering into his chest. "Gram, you love him more than me. You wouldn't beat him."

"Pshaw. Everyone knows you love your grandbabies more. But, shhh, don't go telling him that. He'll feel bad." Her west Texas accent cut through the lines, familiar and true to her home state.

"I won't tell him."

"Of course not. You know which side your biscuit's buttered. Speaking of food. Have you had a decent meal?"

"Yes, ma'am. I ate at a place called The Maple Pit today. The food was almost as good as yours." He licked his lips, imagining the meatloaf.

"High praise coming from you. What'd ya eat?"

He told her about his meal, making sure to let her know how delicious it all was. If Delaney wanted to kick him out of her town, he'd be tempted to stay for the food alone.

"That sounds great. I wish I could get their recipe."

"Well, Jones's wife works there. Maybe I can pull a favor." *Not after you give your speech.* True, he should have asked before.

"Don't go through no trouble for me. I can fiddle around the kitchen and come up with my own recipe."

"I know you can, Gram." A beeping noise from the background grabbed his attention. "What's that?"

"Cupcakes are ready. Marla needed some for her kid's birthday party, so I volunteered. You know she's dealing with chemo."

"Yes, ma'am. You mentioned it." His grandmother would cook for the whole town if they let her. "Give her my best and I'll talk to you later, Gram."

"Be sure you do."

With a good-bye, he ended the call.

Tonight's conversation with Delaney wasn't going to be easy. Hopefully, God would hear his and his grandmother's prayers. Maybe even give him a pass. No, he didn't deserve one.

If you made a mistake, you should have to suffer the consequences. Wasn't that a part of growing up and taking responsibility for your screw ups? Of course, Gram said his guilt was punishment enough.

Was it?

Raising twin boys alone because of his actions...well, guilt was a good reminder to stay on the straight and narrow. However, it wouldn't ease Delaney's suffering. Her family would never be the same. But then again, her family wasn't the only one his actions had impacted.

Humidity clogged her airway as Delaney walked toward a park bench. A bead of sweat rolled down her t-shirt, forcing the material to cling to her skin. Didn't the sun get the memo that it was close to seven? The summer day seemed to stretch in front of her along with its intense heat. Sitting down and resting sounded wonderful right about now.

Business at The Pit had increased the last hour of her shift. Her feet ached in her shoes, her toes dying to wiggle with freedom. Sure, she was thankful for the boom the restaurant experienced.

Not too long ago a foreclosure had loomed over them. Today's steady flow of customers prevented her from dwelling on the impending conversation with Luke.

Only now, there was nothing but the call of birds and the noise of the cicadas to occupy her thoughts. Ones that centered on a handsome Texan with ominous news. Or was her mind just jumping to the negative?

A low rumble of a motorcycle startled her. She turned in time to see it roll to a stop. The rider rose and took off his helmet in one fluid motion. It was almost like watching a commercial or a scene from a movie.

Luke certainly had the rugged and handsome part down pat.

He spotted her, then his steps faltered.

Did she make him as nervous as he made her? The thought offered a small measure of comfort.

She stopped on the trail, waiting for him to catch up. His long strides brought him to her side in no time. A waft of Irish Spring filled her senses. No cologne, just soap.

Somehow that was more potent than the fragrant liquid could ever be.

"Hey, you're here." He gave a half smile, although it seemed a bit forced and a tad shaky.

"Right on time. I know how you military types are." A chuckle escaped, bobbing his Adam's apple. She blinked. They were here about Parker and nothing more.

Get it together, Dee.

She was too old to let a man turn her into a mushy pile of hormones. "Should we go sit somewhere?" She met his gaze and froze. What was it about his cool blue eyes that made her heart head for her stomach?

Luke Robinson was the opposite of Parker in every way. Race, looks, personality. Parker had been on the reserved side and about an inch shorter than her six-foot frame. Luke, however, seemed confident and borderline cocky. He had at least three inches on her, and she couldn't stop looking at him. "Yes, ma'am."

She raised an eyebrow.

"Delaney." His voice came out slightly raspy. He covered his mouth and cleared his throat.

Okay, not *that* cocky.

"Lead the way, please."

"All right." A barrier between them was much needed. Forgetting her desire to sit on a bench, Dee headed for the picnic table. She wasn't sure what was going on, but her hormones were out of control.

It would have been comical if it didn't induce such a panic. She hadn't felt like this since she met Parker, and now a fellow soldier elicited a similar reaction.

A shiver slithered down her spine. There was no way she could go down the path of a soldier's wife again. Not that she was thinking about marriage. Some things were deal breakers. She couldn't do that to herself.

Let alone her boys.

No. *If* she ever did enter the dating scene again, it would be to someone steady and dependable. Whose job had no hazards to their wellbeing?

Doesn't sound very exciting.

She ignored her inner voice and sat across from Luke. He settled down, fingers tented on top of the table. "So, what's up?" She tried to lace calm and cool into her voice but failed miserably.

"Ever since Jones's death, I've had a rough time of it."

Her heart dipped in a familiar ache. "I understand."

"How could you?" Luke shook his head, disgust lining his features. "What I feel nowhere compares to what you feel. You were married to him. Have two kids by him."

"True, but you worked with him." She bit her lip. "When I first found out, grief overwhelmed me. I literally thought about nothing but myself for the first year. I'm sorry to say, I didn't even think of what his old platoon would have felt."

"No." He held his hands up. "You have nothing to be sorry for. We didn't pledge our lives to him, just to protect him. And we failed. I failed."

"No, don't say that." Her hand reached out on its own accord, resting on top of his. "You can't be responsible for every soldier who doesn't come back. It's not your job."

"But—"

She shook her head. Misplaced guilt was worse than survivor's guilt in her opinion. There was no reason for Luke Robinson to suffer. No, they had all suffered enough. "No, repeat after me. It's not my job, it's God's."

"I know it's God's job, but we all have some culpability on this earth." He squeezed her hand and let go. "Me most of all."

"So am I responsible for letting him go off to war? For failing to convince him to not reenlist? He would've been home with me and my kids instead of in some stupid helicopter."

"No," a groan of frustration ripped from his lips. He ran a hand over his hair. "Please, let me finish."

She nodded.

"I was new to the unit. It was my second week there. I deployed as a replacement. Only that day, I got sick. Food poisoning. It was supposed to be me on that helicopter. Not Jones. Me." The last word came out in a stark whisper.

Chill bumps raced up Delaney's arms despite June's high temperature and the bright sun. "What are you saying?"

Luke swallowed, his Adam's apple moving with the movement. His blue eyes had darkened, his brow furrowed with heartache. "I'm saying I'm the reason your husband died. He took my place while I lay in the sick bay. I'm the reason you're a widow."

Silence roared in her ears. Her forehead beaded with perspiration as his words sunk in. Parker wasn't supposed to be on that helicopter. She tried to catch her breath as her vision clouded with unshed tears.

He wasn't supposed to be on the helicopter.

A tear slipped free.

"I'm so sorry. I can't tell you enough how much I wish I could go backward in time. Believe me, I'd trade my life for his in a heartbeat."

She nodded, hearing words but not their meaning.

Parker wasn't supposed to be on the helicopter.

Instead, he'd taken Luke Robinson's fate.

Chapter Three

Time froze. The heartache on her face tore Luke's heart apart. For a moment, he had wanted to accept the out she offered. That it wasn't his fault. Yet, to do so would go against everything he'd learned over the past three years.

While Delaney was bound by the hold of depression, he'd been wrapped up in the contents of Jim Bean and Hennessey.

It wasn't until his chain of command gave him an ultimatum that he realized he had landed in an abyss of darkness and self-pity. With his friend's help and the grace of God, he began to climb up from the pit of his own doing.

His relationship with the Almighty was a silver lining. It was the reason he needed to atone and right his wrongs. God gave him the strength to tell Delaney the real reason she was a widow.

Right now, the deafening silence was killing him. The pounding in his ears was making him nauseous. "Please say something." The words came out hoarse.

Delaney blinked and tears slid down her cheeks. "I don't know what to say."

"I get that." He swallowed around the lump in his throat.

What was she supposed to tell the person who inadvertently killed her spouse? He'd be speechless as well. "I want you to know that I have a month of leave from the Army." He splayed his hands. "I'm at your disposal. If you need repairs fixed…anything, you name it."

"To atone for your sins?" The question hovered in the air. There was no malice in her voice only massive amounts of confusion.

"I know nothing will bring him back, but I feel the need to do something. To make sure you and your boys are okay." The ache increased in his chest.

Would the pressure ever release? He thought the truth would set him free. Only it left an ache, with the weight of an anvil, sitting on his chest.

Inescapable.

Undeniable.

"I…I need to process this." Delaney stood, refusing to look him in the face.

"Okay." He watched her. Each emotion flitting over her face reminded him of an unraveling thread.

"I'm leaving." She grabbed her purse.

"Are you okay to drive?" He stood, worry clawing up his insides. "Should I call someone? I could even drive you."

She shook her head, her long black hair swinging with the movement. She wiped her face, but more tears came. "No. I'm fine to drive. You just…you just stay here. I'll call you or something."

With that, she whirled around, her long legs eating up the distance between the bench and the parking lot. He sank down onto the bench seat.

Finding Love

That was *nothing* like any of the scenarios he'd played out in his head.
Yelling? Yes.
Slap in the face? Yes.
Crying and then leaving? Not so much.
He rubbed his forehead. *What now, Lord?* He couldn't stay out here until her shock wore off. Yet, he didn't know what else to do. With no hint of a sunset near, the sun continued its job of illumination and warmth as if it hadn't witnessed their scene.
With a sigh, Luke got up from the picnic bench. It wasn't like she was coming back any time soon.
Maybe now was the time to head to the B&B and attempt sleep. Hopefully by morning the shock would wear off, and Delaney would give him an idea of what he should do with the rest of his leave.
When he arrived at the B&B, Ms. Bella moved from the stovetop to the counter and back, flitting around like a hummingbird. Her petite frame was engulfed by her floral skirt and apron.
The bun on the top of her head looked bigger than her face.
"*Buonasera*, Luke."
"Evening, Ms. Bella."
"You eat?"
"No, ma'am." He shook his head and sat down at the table situated in the breakfast nook. Crossing his feet at the ankles, he leaned back, watching her movements. Back and forth she went from the island to the stockpot on the stove. It amazed him.
When he first arrived, she informed him her kitchen was always open because she was always in it. She wasn't kidding.
"How come you didn't eat?" Her thick Italian accent added charm and vitality to her tone.

"I forgot, ma'am."

"Big robust guy like you?" She tutted and shook her head.

Ms. Bella flicked the pasta into the boiling water. The smell of bread curled around him, awakening his stomach.

"How come? You worried?"

"A little." He shrugged, hoping the gesture would prevent further questions. No need to bare his soul. He'd already met that quota for the day.

"You pray?"

An easy grin filled his face. "All the time."

"Good. That's what you should do. It says pray without…hmmm, what's the word?"

"Ceasing."

"*Sì*. Pray without ceasing, and you will be okay."

"Sometimes, the waiting is the worst."

"*Sì*. But the Bible tells us to wait on the Lord, Luke."

Why did it have to be so hard? His mouth could form a prayer faster than he could tie his shoe laces, but the worry wasn't so easy to dissolve. *Lord, help my unbelief.* He exhaled, imagining the worry escaping in his breath, and tried to focus on the joy on Bella's face as she prepared dinner.

Once the food was on the table, he bowed his head and said a prayer for the food, the hands that prepared it, and for Delaney.

Always, Delaney.

Meeting her had jumbled his insides to resemble an anagram. The sadness that lingered in her eyes twisted the knife of guilt.

When she was just Jones's widow, he allowed himself to believe life treated her kindly. That she was living well on the Army widow benefits and surrounded by friends and family who would take care of her.

Seeing her in person though...

It was like his soul recognized a part of hers. Of course, that was completely ridiculous. If he hadn't known he was sober, he'd question his line of thinking. A sigh escaped as he took a bite of the pasta.

Now that he'd met her, his desire to *know*, with all certainty, that she was okay had increased. That she wasn't merely surviving, but thriving. How could he do that? Would she let him after today's announcement?

"Why do you care so much?" he whispered.

"What did you say, Luke?"

He glanced up, remembering he was in Ms. Bella's kitchen. "I was just talking to myself. I have a lot on my mind."

Ms. Bella leaned on the counter and looked him in the eyes, her green eyes flashing. "If you have girl trouble, you pray harder. Tell her you're sorry, and you'll do anything to fix it. And then you do it. She'll come around." She patted him on the shoulder. "Eat."

"Yes, ma'am."

After dinner, Luke sat on the part of the porch that overlooked an empty field. There was no fence or enclosure, nothing but wide open spaces. It reminded him a little of Texas but greener and with more trees.

Okay, so maybe it was nothing like Texas.

Regardless, it made him think of home.

The sky was a mix of blues. Navy coated the top as the bottom slipped into a range of blues. Darkness slowly shrouded the light. Was it a sign?

Lord, I want to fix Delaney's pain, but I know I can't. There's nothing I can do to reverse Jones's death. He's gone. Luke rubbed his eyes. *I just don't understand why You didn't let me get on that helicopter. What could You possibly want with me?*

Delaney's face flashed in his mind. The heartache that etched on her face at his words would be the death of him. Never again did he want to cause her pain like that.

Am I here to help her in some way? Is that why you saved me?

No, that made no sense. How could keeping him alive and not her actual husband work out? He groaned. If he kept these thoughts up he was going to drive himself insane…or worse, to a bottle.

Lord, please guide me. I have no idea what to do. How to help her. I'm not even sure she wants my help, Lord. Yet, I know you called me out here for her benefit. Please bring wisdom and clarity soon, before I climb the walls. And please keep me from temptation. Amen.

―

Dessert.

It was the only thing that was going to ease the heartache that had taken up residence with one confession from Luke Robinson's lips. Delaney walked into her childhood kitchen.

The one that had been filled with laughter from her parents and her older brother. The one she left on the throes of love and with hopes of creating the same atmosphere.

Now, she was back as a widow, living with her mother.

She paused. Why was it so dark? Usually her mother had multiple lights on in the house. It was enough to make a person cringe at the over usage of electricity. Thoughts of maple baked goodness pushed the cares of electricity to the back of her mind.

A flick of the switch flooded the kitchen with light. The sunken bulbs gleamed, chasing out darkness.

"Ah!" Her mother screamed.

"Good grief, Ma!" She pressed a hand to her heart. "What are you doing here in the dark?"

Her mother looked at her with a tear-stained face and a silver, picture frame clutched to her chest. "Just thinking."

She walked toward her mother, wrapping an arm around her. Apparently she wasn't the only one reeling from the trials of life. Her mother held out the frame so she could see.

The smiling faces of her mom and dad on their wedding day greeted her. How had her mom been able to view the picture in the dark?

"Missing Daddy?"

"Like crazy." Her mother sniffed. "It's amazing how the grief just appears out of nowhere."

"Ain't that the truth," she replied softly.

"Of course, *you* understand."

She nodded and stepped out of the hug. Whoever thought she would be united with her mother by widowhood? Though depressing, it forged a bond between them that couldn't be denied.

A blessing from the tragedy. She shook her head trying to dispel the thoughts and images of a flag-draped coffin. Her breath caught as she tried to push the memories back.

"So what did Luke want?"

Curiosity laced her mother's voice, but there was a hint of something else. She met her mother's gaze. Did she know how much the man affected her?

"To atone for his sins."

"What do you mean?"

Tears swam in her eyes. "He was the reason Parker was on the helicopter." She wiped a tear away. "Apparently Parker took his spot because Luke got sick." Just saying the words aloud made her stomach dip in protest.

"Oh, Dee." Her mother's sigh was audible. "I made maple bacon cheesecake." Her mother offered a sympathetic smile.

"I'll take a slice." *Or two.*

Her mother wrapped her in another hug then got up. "Nothing soothes the ache better than a slice of cheesecake."

"Normally I would disagree, but today, that's just the kind of mood I'm in."

"Oh, Delaney, you need to relax. Having dessert every now and again won't hurt you."

"Tell that to my hips," she smirked.

Her mother laughed, all traces of her tears gone. "We got the same hips, Dee. You'll be just fine."

The first bite was like heaven. The explosion of flavors on her tongue made her grin in delight. Desserts generally made her happy, but maple bacon cheesecake was pure bliss.

Then again, her mother could make any dessert and Delaney would be floating on the proverbial cloud.

"Do you want to talk about why you're so upset?"

Bits of cheesecake sputtered as the ridiculous nature of her mother's question hit her gut. "It's Parker we're talking about, Ma."

"I understand that, Dee. But how is getting sick Luke's fault?"

Finding Love

It wasn't, but that didn't make hearing the news any better. Instead of responding, she took another bite and shrugged.

"Did you tell him he had misplaced guilt?"

She snorted. "Before he said he was the reason Parker got on that helicopter." She explained further at the look of confusion on her mother's face.

"Poor boy. I can't imagine the guilt he's been carrying around." Her mother pointed a finger. "You need to tell him to let it go and that you forgive him. Let him move on with his life."

How could she when she wasn't even sure how she felt about his admission. She balanced her fork back and forth on her fingers. *Parker wasn't supposed to be on the helicopter!* "I don't know if I can, Ma."

"You will. You just make sure you keep the lines of communication open, huh?"

"Why?" The words slipped free before she could recall them, but since they were out in the open, she forged on. "He can go back to Texas, and life can go back to normal."

Her mother's laughter rang loud and clear. "Sweetie, don't be delusional. I'm not God, but even I can see things will never be the same for you again." With that, she headed out of the kitchen.

What does she mean by that?

As her thoughts rambled back and forth, bites of her dessert slowly disappeared. She tapped the tines against her lips. On the one hand, she knew Luke wasn't to blame.

The terrorist who fired the RPG had killed him. Yet the other part of her, the one who still couldn't believe Parker was gone, hurt. Ached to lash out and demand why.

Why, Lord? Why did you have to take him from me? We were supposed to grow old and gray together. Not this. A tear slid down her face. *I shouldn't be raising my kids alone. They no longer have a father to shape them into manhood. We live with my mother now. This wasn't the plan.*

A picture of Luke's strong face entered her mind. The anguish in his voice had been real as he related what happened. She imagined he experienced survivor's guilt, since no one survived the crash.

The fact that he was supposed to be on it had been enough to tear his world apart. Even though he expressed remorse, she wasn't sure if she could offer words of forgiveness, but a conversation between them would have to happen.

How else could she convince him to go back to Texas and leave her alone?

Chapter Four

The smells in The Maple Pit were even better at breakfast than they were at dinner. He couldn't help but watch as the cooks moved in harmony. Plates appeared on the serving counter, overflowing with goodness.

Piles of waffles sprinkled with bits of bacon and confectioner's sugar sat in perfection. The aromas seemed to dance in the air. And he had no choice but to wait patiently. Luke took a sip of his black coffee as he imagined how his order of maple French toast would taste.

Normally, he didn't eat such a sugary meal, but when in Rome, right?

"Here you go." He looked up to thank his server and met the gaze of Delaney. The overwhelming sense of déjà vu swamped his senses.

He laced his words with caution, "Good morning." Although he knew she worked here, he wasn't prepared to see her first thing. Besides, didn't she work the dinner shift? He went ahead and voiced his thoughts aloud.

"I do. I was doing something else, saw you and offered to bring your food." She laid her hands on the counter top, fiddling with the edge of a napkin.

Suddenly he didn't feel like eating. The thought must have showed on his face because Delaney offered a small smile.

"Eat. I promise it's good."

"I believe it. Just don't feel hungry all of a sudden." He gulped. Why had he told her the truth? *Why can't you keep your mouth shut?*

Her lips turned downward. "About that."

"Please. I know you're not ready to talk."

"How can you tell?" Her brown eyes darkened in disbelief.

"You look like you're going to shred that napkin to pieces."

She looked down, noticing the napkin in her hand. A wry grin transformed her face, taking his breath away. He grabbed the mug to refocus his thoughts. *Not yours, Robinson.*

"Okay, so maybe I don't want to talk about it. However, I think we need to."

"All right. What do you want to say?"

"Were you the only one with food poisoning?"

He blinked. *What?* "I…" His mind had lost the words necessary to communicate. "No, I wasn't."

"How many other guys had it?"

"Two others."

"So three people took y'all's spots?"

His mind tripped at the 'y'all.' He didn't even know Virginians said the word, although it sounded a lot different than the way a Texan would. "Yes, ma'am."

"Don't 'ma'am' me, Luke Robinson."

His eyes widened at the rebuke.

"How do you know Parker took your spot?"

"I..." his voice trailed off and he looked away. He couldn't finish his thought. Didn't want to see her face when he said what he had to say. It was too difficult.

"Luke? What aren't you saying?"

He ran a hand over his face and looked around. "Maybe we should do this somewhere else?"

She nodded slowly. "Come with me."

He followed her to a back hallway. A long corridor was filled with closed doors. She paused at one and opened it. After peering in, she closed it and moved down to the next one.

This time she knocked and waited for a response.

"Come in," a female voice called out.

Delaney pushed the door open. "Hey, Nina. Can I borrow your office for a few minutes? It's important."

"Sure."

Luke leaned around the doorframe in time to see a petite Black woman come around her desk. She was so tiny it was almost laughable. He looked between Delaney and the woman. *Couldn't be sisters.*

"Where are the babies?" Delaney asked.

"Kandi has them."

"She's so great with them."

"Tell me about it," Nina replied.

Luke stepped back allowing room for her to pass. She scrutinized him and then turned back to Delaney. "I'll be up front. Come get me when you're done."

"All right." Delaney looked at him and gestured inside.

Suddenly, privacy didn't seem like such a good idea. He did *not* need to be in a small space with her. Not where he could clearly smell the scent of her perfume, or maybe it was shower gel.

The tantalizing smell of strawberries pulled at his gut.

Not yours, Robinson. Focus, man.

Delaney closed the door and leaned back against it. "Talk."

He gulped. "I have no clue which person took my spot. Like you said, I wasn't the only one who got sick."

"Then why the need to make amends?"

"Because someone was on that plane because of me!" The shout tore free, ripped from his gut as if he were reliving the news all over again.

Three additional men had been on that helicopter. Any one of them would still be alive if he had been on it instead.

"Luke," Delaney breathed out his name. Empathy flooded her face.

He turned so he couldn't see the look in her eyes. She had no right to treat him with such grace.

"Luke, look at me." Her voice was stronger, authoritative even.

His body betrayed him and he met her warm brown eyes.

"You can't atone for something you had no control over. *Plus*, you can't be so sure that Parker was the one who took your spot. This line of thinking is so misguided. If you truly believe you were at fault, you'd have to go visit the other two guys' families."

"I already have."

Her eyes widened. "Are you serious?"

He nodded, trying to find the rest of the words to finish this conversation. His insides were tearing apart. "Last year I saw one family. Worked on their farm for two weeks."

"Seriously?"

"Yes, ma–" he paused, trying to stop the ma'am at the arch of her eyebrow. "Earlier this year I went to the other family. They kicked me off their property. So, I sent them my paycheck."

"Then why offer me a month of your time?"

"You have two boys."

"Wow."

Was wow a good thing or a bad thing?

His hands found their way into his pockets, clenching in a fist now that they were unseen. Nerves tightened the muscles in his body.

Whatever was going through her mind…well, he wasn't entirely sure he wanted to know, but he didn't want her to send him away. The desire to stay, to take care of her amazed him.

His only question was: *is it misplaced guilt or something more?*

Delaney placed a hand on her forehead. "I need time to think."

"I won't leave until you tell me to," he answered quietly.

Something flashed in her eyes. He wished he knew her well enough to understand what that look meant.

"We should go. I'm sure Nina has work to do."

He grabbed a sticky note off the desk and wrote his cell number before handing it to her. "Call me when you've decided your next steps. I'll answer no matter the time."

Taking a deep breath, he brushed past her and walked away. Yet for some strange reason, he felt like he left a piece of himself behind.

The noise of The Maple Pit couldn't distract Delaney from the tumult of emotions her mind was putting her through. She'd been prepared to feel anger at Luke's bombshell.

Only the hits kept coming. He wasn't the only one who'd been sick.

And he visited every single family who lost someone.

The thought dropped her heart to her toes. How could she maintain her resentment when the man was trying to atone to all possible parties?

His kindness infuriated her.

"Dee?"

She looked up.

Nina's brow furrowed with concern. "Can I sit with you?"

"Sure." It wasn't like she needed the other seat.

Did Luke finish his food? Her head swiveled to the bar. He sat there, pushing his food around on his plate. Even in his misery his good looks couldn't be denied.

"Who is that, Delaney?"

"Oh, um...he knew Parker." She tore her eyes away from Luke to meet her sister-in-law's gaze.

"Did something happen?"

Delaney leaned forward and spilled her guts.

When she first met Nina, she assumed the woman was a gold digger out to get Dwight in her clutches. Only it turned out her brother answered an ad in the newspaper to marry Nina for money.

Somedays the whole scenario still blew her mind. Yet, the two were still going strong after a year and a half of marriage. Plus, she was now an aunt to twins: a niece and a nephew.

"What are you going to do?" Nina asked.

"I have no idea. Part of me says I should send him back to Texas. I mean really, what could he do? Our house doesn't need any repairs. I don't own a farm." She shook her head.

"Then tell him he doesn't owe you anything and poof..." Nina made a disappearing motion with her hands.

But I can't! The idea of him leaving bothered her more than it should.

She inhaled a shaky breath. "I don't know if I should. I don't understand it, but I don't think that's the answer."

"Have you prayed?"

"No," she admitted in exasperation. "My brain has been so addled; I didn't even think of it."

"Let's do that now."

Delaney bowed her head as Nina offered up a prayer. "Lord, please give Delaney the wisdom she needs for this situation. Only You know the right thing to do. Please make it clear for her. In Jesus' Name, Amen."

"Amen." She squeezed Nina's hands. "Thank you so much."

"Anytime."

A change in the subject was needed. "How are your babies?"

"Gabe's teething."

"Already?"

Nina nodded her head vigorously. "I'm not ready for them to get teeth. How do you handle the boys growing?"

Delaney smiled. Preston and Philip were nine going on thirty. Philip was an old soul and Preston was always bouncing off the walls. "Just hug them tight until they let go. It eases the ache. Is Abby teething too?"

"No, thank goodness. I'm thankful the twin thing doesn't necessarily mean they'll reach milestones at the same time."

"It's so true. Preston has always reached milestones before Philip, but I think Philip is more mature."

"Hey, he's leaving, Delaney."

Her eyes locked onto Luke's tall figure as he headed for the door. She wanted to call out, to stop him. But indecision rendered her mute. She still had no idea what to do about him. "I have his number."

"Are you going to call him?"

"Whenever I figure out what to do." *Tell him to stay.* She stood abruptly. "I gotta go. The boys will be done with swim lessons soon."

"Okay. Are you dropping them off at the house before your shift tonight?"

She nodded. Kandi, Nina's eighteen-year-old adopted daughter, babysat them when her mother was unable to or needed a break. Thankfully, Kandi was always happy to help out.

"See you later."

As soon as she picked up her boys, their chatter filled the car. Preston was excited because he swam in the deep end without floaties.

"You should have seen it, Mom. I looked like an eel."

"An eel? Why not a fish."

"Fish aren't cool enough."

She chuckled. "What about you Philip, did you enjoy the lesson?"

"It was okay," he said with a shrug.

Preston turned to Philip and began to talk his ear off. Sometimes she wondered if Philip ever wanted to hide from his younger brother. Even though their age difference was in minutes and not years, it was enough to give Preston the characteristics of the baby of the family.

Her Bluetooth chimed, signaling a call from her mom.

"Hey, Ma. What's up?"

"Dwight's been in a car accident."

"What? Is he...?" Her stomach clenched, hovering in the pit of fear that an injury phone call brought with it.

"He's okay, Delaney. He broke his arm, but that's all."

Relief flooded through her. "Did you tell Nina?"

"I did. She's on the way to the hospital. I called Alex and asked him if he could stay and cook."

"Can he?" Alex was the other chef besides her mother and brother.

"Yes, but we'll still need another person back there."

An image of Luke popped in her brain. *No. What were the odds he knew how to cook?* "What if I can find one?"

"That would be great. Call me as soon as you can. I need to know if we should close the doors today."

"All right."

Delaney put the car in park in front of the house. She turned and met her twins' concerned faces. The boys' puppy dog expressions tugged at her heart.

"Is Uncle D going to be okay?" Worry laced Philip's words.

"He is, buddy. Don't worry." She reached a hand back and he slid his hand into hers. She gave it a squeeze. "How about we go inside and get a snack?" While she figured out how to ask Luke if he knew how to cook.

The boys headed into the step-down living room which was situated across from the kitchen. Last year, Dwight had paid for a remodel and now it supported brown granite countertops.

A matching island gorgeously graced the center of the room. It was the perfect place to make a fruit salad for their snack.

Dee grabbed some strawberries and tossed them with blueberries and bananas. After placing two bowls in front of the boys, who were glued to the screen watching cartoons, she headed back toward the kitchen. Now that they were occupied, she could call Luke.

It's now or never.

"Hello."

Her pulse raced as his voice crossed the line. How did it manage to sound deeper? "Luke, it's Delaney."

"I know."

Duh. "I have a question for you."

"Shoot."

"Do you know how to cook?"

"Yes, my grandmother taught me. She's the best cook in west Texas." The pride in his voice was unmistakable…and endearing. "Why? Do you need a cook?"

"Yes, my brother's the chef at The Pit, and he broke his arm."

Chapter Five

Luke's heart thudded in his chest. Delaney needed him. He couldn't believe it. Then again, desperate measures and all that. "If someone's available to show me what to do, I'll do it."

"Thank you so much." The relief in her voice was palpable. It came through loud and clear.

"By any chance are you vaccinated for Hepatitis A?"

"I can check my military shot record. They give us shots for all sorts of weird things." He was old school and traveled with his shot records and his leave paperwork. His finger scrolled down the paperwork. "Yes, I am."

"Great." A light laugh escaped. "I'm so glad you can help out."

"When do I need to get there?"

"Now if possible. Alex—he's the other chef—will be there to talk you through it. My mother's with Dwight now and his wife is on the way. Then I'm sure my mother will work tonight, but dinner on a Friday is usually packed. They'll need the extra hand."

He could do this. *Lord, please help me do this.* Cooking with his grandmother for their local church was entirely different than cooking dinner at a restaurant. "I'll leave now."

"Thank you, Luke."

"It's what I'm here for." *Delaney*, went unspoken. As much as he wanted to say her name, he was afraid emotions he didn't want to examine would reveal themselves. It was safer if it just went unspoken.

They said their goodbyes and he grabbed his wallet and cell. Driven with purpose, his long strides ate up the distance between the B&B and his bike.

The Harley barely had time to warm up before he drove into the parking lot of The Pit. Already, there was a steady stream of cars in the paved lot. Dismounting he headed inside. *Lord, please let this go smoothly.*

The redhead was back.

Every time he walked into The Maple Pit it felt like a scene from *Groundhog Day*. Did everyone maintain the same smile and space?

Yet, a second glance showed him that some of the servers were different. The crowd had a couple of familiar faces but new ones were present as well.

He couldn't deny the relaxing atmosphere of The Pit. It reminded him of family dinners at home. Laughter floated, mingling in with the sound of Christian music playing over the speakers.

The tablecloths and mason jar centerpieces added a touch of class but kept the homey feel. The Williamses had a great thing going for them.

"Hi again. Do you want to eat at the bar?" The redhead beamed his way.

"Not today." But if he ever did have to eat at the bar, he knew he would be fine. Apparently, the bar was strictly for looks. The Pit didn't serve alcohol. "Actually, I'm looking for Alex. Delaney needs an extra cook."

Confusion marred her features. "What?" The phone at the hostess station rang. "Just a second."

A series of "oh nos" and "uh-huhs" filled the silence. Finally, she hung up. "That was Delaney. She wants me to introduce you to Alex."

"Lead the way." He gestured toward the kitchen area.

"I'm Nikki by the way."

"Luke Robinson, but you can call me Robinson."

"Military?"

"Yes, ma'am. Army."

"Thank you for your service."

He dipped his head in acknowledgment. The nerve endings on his body grew taut. He didn't have the mental fortitude to make small talk. Not with so much hanging in the balance. It was like he was auditioning for Delaney's approval.

What would happen if he botched this job?

Why did it matter so much?

"Alex," Nikki called out. She rolled her eyes as a slender man, wearing earbuds, steadily chopped bell peppers. She reached out and tapped him on the shoulder.

The man never broke stride. Once the bell pepper was complete, he slipped off the headphones and turned toward Nikki.

"I heard you, just don't like stopping mid chop."

"Understood." She pointed to Luke. "This is Robinson. Dwight broke his arm in a car accident. Delaney wants him to help you back here."

"You cook before?" Alex asked, black eyebrows raised in skepticism. His olive skin and black hair were indicative of his Latin heritage.

"Yes. My grandmother taught me. We usually bake for church crowds or those needing meals delivered to them."

"All right, let's see what you got."

For the next hour, he cooked while Alex watched. The recipes were easy to follow and after a while, he found his rhythm. By dinner time, Luke was comfortable in the kitchen.

Thankfully, Alex didn't give him any big meal items or recipes he could ruin. It helped knowing what was expected of him.

"Hey, how's everything?"

He turned at the sound of Delaney's voice.

Luke paused. Her beauty stunned him. The simple jeans and white t-shirt should have looked frumpy. Nevertheless, his brain still shorted as if she was wearing an evening gown.

The way her hair was pulled into a ponytail drew attention to the shape of her eyes and her prominent cheekbones. He cleared his throat. "All right."

"Thank you again for doing this." She squeezed his arm, then quickly let it go.

Judging from the heat emanating from his arm, she'd felt the spark as well. "You know I'll do anything for you." Heat flushed his face. "I mean to help out...because I owe you."

Delaney laughed, the sound light and airy. "I know what you meant, Luke."

"That's a relief."

She cocked her head. "Are you adding 'ma'am' in your head?"

His mouth dropped open in shock. *How did she know that?*

"Judging by the wide-eyed shock, that's a yes. I thought we agreed I'd call you Luke and you'd call me Delaney."

"We did."

She looked at him expectantly. When he said nothing she leaned forward, cupping her ear.

"Delaney." The words were pried from his lips and sent a tremor of awareness down his spine. He stepped back. "I need to get to work, boss lady."

To think her family *owned* The Pit. He'd never known anyone who ran a restaurant.

"That's still not my name, but I'll leave. I've got tables to serve." She sauntered off.

"Wow, I've never seen Delaney behave like that."

Luke turned to Alex, who looked bemused. "Like what? She's not friendly to y'all?"

"No, she's nice. All of them are. That just looked a little more than nice, if you get my drift." Alex chuckled and turned back to his station.

Just how loud was the music in his ears?

Luke stared through the kitchen opening, watching as Delaney greeted a table. He got the feeling that she was uneasy around him. Never would he have attributed her behavior to flirting.

Was it possible she was interested in him? Could he actually pray for something like that?

No. He was here to make amends. Not poach on another man's territory.

Even if he's no longer living?

Unease rolled through him. What an appalling thought. The fact that it was the truth didn't make it any better.

*Lord, help me to remember why I'm here. I'm here to help, not get my heart tangled up in...*he paused, searching for the right word. Whatever the word was, he didn't want to experience it. This was about making things right, not receiving a kickback for himself.

The smell of the pulled pork with maple barbecue sauce elicited a rumble of expectation from Delaney's stomach. She was so glad it was time for a break.

The employee room was devoid of all noise except for the sound coming from the little TV in the corner. She pulled a chair in front of her to prop her feet up. It might be time to get a new pair of shoes.

Lately, her feet constantly screamed in protest. The door creaked open and noise from the restaurant filtered in. She turned and froze.

Luke.

He had a plate of food and a drink. *Great.* She never imagined they would have a break together. His eyes locked onto hers. Was it her imagination or did he look uncertain?

Emotion seemed to alter the tint of his blue eyes. Eyes she could stare into any time of day.

Where did that come from?

The feelings coursing through her unnerved her. If she would have sighed aloud, it couldn't have surprised her more. She blinked and stared at her plate. Luke Robinson was dangerous to her peace of mind.

How could she be saddened and angry over Parker's needless death and mooning over the handsome Texan in her next breath?

So exasperating.
Disloyal even.

"How's your shift going?" Luke asked as he pulled a chair out on the other side of the table.

"Pretty good. It can be tiring when it's crowded, but it also helps the time pass."

He nodded and then bowed his head, his lips moving in a soundless prayer.

You're a Christian?

The sight of him blessing his food made her stomach dip. Yes, he mentioned atonement of sins, but she thought that was some Texan or military honor code. Was that what fueled his decision to seek her out as some type of penance?

Would God require that of a person?

An audible "amen" graced his lips. He looked up and stared straight at her. His gaze was so direct she had to wonder if he didn't hear her thoughts.

She licked her lips, trying to think of something to say. "Are you doing okay in the kitchen?"

"Yes, Alex is a good teacher."

"Oh, good. Thanks again for the help. I know Dwight will be grateful once he's off pain killers."

"How is he?"

"All right, considering. I think it shook up Nina and me more than anything. It's not the first time he's broken a bone, but the first because of a car accident."

"You and Dwight are close?" His eyes searched hers.

"Yes. We're twins."

His eyebrows rose, lines creasing his forehead. "Twins? What was that like?"

"Chaos," she said with a laugh. "We were always up to no good, as my mom liked to call it." She took a bite of her food now that the tension abated.

"I always wondered what it would be like to have a brother or sister."

She dabbed her mouth with the cloth napkin. "You're an only child?"

"Mmm hmm. It was a little lonely, but I did have a horse." His blue eyes crinkled with amusement.

"I've always wanted to go horseback riding, but I'm too scared." *Great, why did I have to tell him that?*

"I could take you."

The strength in his voice shot an arrow of awareness through her body. "Thanks for the offer, but summer time is pretty busy for me. With the boys out of school, I have to make sure I have a full line of activities or they'll die from boredom."

She thought of Philip and Preston's antics when there was nothing to do. Dee chuckled under her breath. Life would never be boring with those two.

"You sound like a good mom."

"I hope so."

"I always wanted to know what having a mom was like as well."

Her eyes flew to his face. His words had been matter of fact. No self-pity, no longing. Just facts. *How sad.* "What happened?" she asked softly.

"Car accident when I was two. My grandmother came to live with us after that and, in a sense, raised me."

"I'm so sorry."

He shrugged. "God never promised us easy."

"Amen." She sighed. "My father died five years ago."

"Sorry."

"It's okay. He was there for all the important things. God blessed me in that area." She winced inwardly. Did that sound insensitive considering how young his mom was when she died?

"Death never gets easier."

"Ain't that the truth." She snorted.
Real attractive, Delaney.
Then again, was she trying to be attractive? It's not like she wanted Luke Robinson's attention. She was a widow.
A widow with eyes. The man was seriously good looking, despite his beard-covered face. Normally she didn't do facial hair, but on him, it only added to his appeal.
She took a sip of her tea, hoping to divert her thoughts from his looks.
"Do y'all need me to work tomorrow, too?"
"Probably. I'll double check with my mom."
He nodded. "When do you get a day off?"
"Why?" She blinked. "I'm sorry. I didn't mean to sound rude."
"No apology necessary. I was thinking of taking you on a horseback ride."
"I..." Be alone? With him? *No way.* "That's okay. I'll be with the boys."
"They can come, too."
Her heart stuttered at his suggestion. For some reason, her entire being froze at the thought of introducing him to her kids. "I don't think that's a good idea."
A flash of disappointment crossed his face, but was gone before she could dig deeper into why it bothered her so. Or him.
"Understood." He glanced at his watch. "I need to get back."
"Me, too." She stared at her half eaten dinner. "Guess I'll save this for later."
"You better. I made it."
With a wink, he walked out of the breakroom.

She put a hand over her heart. *Lord, please guard my heart. I'm not ready to enter the dating scene, and I certainly don't want to date another soldier. Take this curiosity…interest…whatever it is, please take it away. I don't want to like him.*

But part of her feared she already did. Despite Luke's good looks and humble personality, his job was a deal breaker for her. There was no way she could devote herself to a relationship that could be ended at the moment of a war cry.

No, she needed to make sure her defenses were up because she *refused* to lose another person, even if it meant she would never find love again.

Chapter Six

The queen-sized bed never felt so good. Luke sighed in relief, glad to rest his bones. He could have sat in the wingback chair situated by the French doors, but it was simply too far away.

His weary body barely avoided bumping into the dresser across from the bed and near the door. Working at The Pit was different than working for Uncle Sam.

The barn had been packed from opening to close. His feet were thankful to get out of his boots once he entered the B&B doors. It had taken every concentrated effort to pull them off and flop backward onto the bed.

Now, if only sleep would come as quickly. Once again, Delaney Jones filled his thoughts.

What was it about her that punched him in the gut? He'd dated before. Been close to marrying even. Yet, none of those women affected him like Delaney. There was something about her that made all his protective instincts come out in full force.

Not only that, but he also wanted to be the one to help her have fun and lighten up. Sorrow clung to her like another layer of skin.

Was it his appearance that brought out the dark cloud? Perhaps she just didn't like strange men who killed her husband. It was obvious she was wary around him, and he couldn't blame her.

The trauma he caused her family was enough to give anyone a sideways glance. Regardless of how he came to Maple Run, he still wanted a chance with her. It took all his will power not to beg her to go out with him.

How was one supposed to handle a situation like this? He rolled into town, told her he was supposed to be on the helicopter, and then…oh, hey, want to go out? He gave a derisive snort.

Finding love wasn't his objective.

All he wanted to do was make amends for his part in Jones's death. Except no one told him how incredibly beautiful Jones's wife was.

He squeezed his eyes shut. His brain couldn't handle the conundrum that was a widowed woman. There should be some manual on navigating those dating waters.

How did you know if she was ready to move on? Plus, she had kids. He'd seen the manual on that, and it wasn't something he wanted to jump into unprepared.

Logically that is.

Emotionally was a different story. His heart sped up in her presence. He felt like a pubescent teen experiencing his first crush. All he could think of was Delaney.

What did she like to do for fun? What could he do to make her notice him? It would have been pathetic and almost humorous if anxiety didn't press so heavily upon him.

He rolled onto his stomach. "I need a diversion, Lord. I can't think about her like this. She's Jones's wife."

Jones isn't here anymore.

The words of Romans scrolled through his mind, "For the woman which hath an husband is bound by the law to her husband so long as he liveth; but if the husband be dead, she is loosed from the law of her husband."

Lord, why can't I reconcile this in my mind? I don't want to do anything outside of Your will. I certainly don't want to express interest and insult her or her late husband. And do I even refer to Jones's as her husband anymore? It's so convoluted, Lord.

He wanted a drink. The feeling coursed through him, hot and swift. With a groan, he picked up his cell phone and dialed his best friend.

"Campbell, here."

"Hey, Soup." Luke said, using his friend's military call sign. "It's Crusoe. How are you?"

"Crusoe! When did you hit stateside?"

"A week ago."

"Where are you?"

"Maple Run, Virginia."

"Virginia? What are you doing there?"

"Making amends. That's not why I called though." He licked his lips. "I want a drink, man."

"Have you prayed?"

He swallowed. "No, dialed your number."

"Let me pray for you." Campbell cleared his throat. "Heavenly Father, we ask that peace would flood Crusoe's soul. Please take temptation away from him and replace it with Your Spirit and truth. In Jesus' Name, Amen."

"Amen," he whispered.

"What brought this on?"

"Jones's wife."

"Okay," Campbell drew out. "What does that mean?"

"I like her, Soup."

"Like *like*?"

"Yep. I know I shouldn't, but I do."

"Why shouldn't you like her?"

"Hello – she's a widow."

"That's right, a widow. I don't mean to sound insensitive, but she's no longer married in the eyes of the Lord. If — and that's on her — if she wanted to start dating, she wouldn't be sinning. Just like you wouldn't be sinning if you started seeing her."

"Then why do I still feel guilty for thinking of her like that?"

"Because you're still blaming yourself for his death. You know as well as I do that things happen. Something comes up and another soldier takes someone else's place. It's part of the job, Crusoe."

"Yeah but Soup, I was supposed to be on that helo."

"And you weren't. God has some purpose for you, man. Blaming yourself is nothing but you doubting God."

His mouth dropped open in shock. He'd never thought of it that way. *Never.* "I…uh…" *have no clue what to say.*

"Hey, man, I get why you're nervous. Dating isn't easy. Being with someone who's been divorced, has kids, or in your case, a widow makes it tougher. But don't look for reasons not to try. If you're truly interested in her, you need to let her know."

He wasn't sure what to think about that, but he appreciated the advice. "Thanks, Soup."

"Anytime, Crusoe, anytime."

Luke hung up, thankful for the wisdom of his friend.

Years ago he'd met Micah Campbell, or Soup as they called him, on a deployment. After Luke suffered an injury, a medevac was called. Micah had been the flight nurse who got him to safety and saw to his injuries. After that, they struck up a friendship.

When his team died in the helicopter crash, grief overcame him. For a year, he spiraled out of control, taking comfort in the bottle. Then another chance meeting during a deployment brought them together.

Micah's steadfast faith had seen him through withdrawals and helped him develop a relationship with God. He owed the man and would help him in any way he could.

Just turned out that tonight he was once again in need of assistance.

He thought about Delaney and her kids. Was he using Jones as an excuse not to get rejected? Because deep down, he expected Delaney to reject him. He had a hand in her husband's death.

He was still in the military.

And he was white.

Okay, so the last one he was unsure of. She didn't seem the type to be racist or reject a guy based on the color of his skin, but he didn't know.

Because you're hiding behind Jones's death.

He ran a hand down his face. Okay, so Soup was right. He was too scared to let her know how he felt. That was something he could pray about. God's answer was sure to be interesting.

"Mom, wake up!"

Delaney groaned as Preston jumped on her bed and shook her body. To think she used to be annoyed by him pulling her eyelids open. At least then, he didn't shake her body like she was a Magic 8 Ball.

"Pres, I'm tired."

"But it's morning time," he whined.

She cracked open an eye to stare at the glass, heart-shaped clock on her nightstand, a one-year-anniversary gift from Parker. The personalized clock was engraved with the statement, 'You have my heart until the end of time.'

For the first month after his death, she'd slept with the thing.

It was barely past six in the morning.

"Pres, it's too early."

"Then why is the sun up?" He peered down into her face, his eyebrows raised in gross exaggeration. His brown puppy dog eyes gleamed against his brown skin as he waited for a response.

"Because it's summer time and it rises early."

"Technically the sun doesn't rise, the earth rotates."

Ugh, smarty pants. "Is your grandmother awake?"

"No, that's why you need to get up. I'm starving." He stretched the last word out to four syllables.

"Is Philip awake?"

Preston snorted. "Of course not, he's buried under his covers." He tugged at her arm trying to pull her out of the bed. "Besides he doesn't have to be awake for you to make breakfast. As soon as you start cooking, he'll wake up."

It was true. Her nine-year-olds were ruled by their stomachs. She'd assumed big appetites wouldn't hit until high school years. Dwight had been constantly hungry as a teen.

Yet, she must have buried the memories of him being a bottomless pit at nine. And to think, God gave her two boys at once.

Double blessing.

Parker had always referred to the boys as a double blessing. He insisted God gave them two because Delaney would be that good of a mom. She had no clue if she was, but she had to get up and make breakfast or risk her arm being pulled out of the socket.

"All right, I'll make breakfast."

"Thank you. I want waffles."

Of course he does.

She stared at him, exasperation trying to wheedle its way in her heart. A morning person she was not.

He clasped his hands holding them underneath his chin. "Please, Mom."

"All right, Pres." How could she resist that adorable face? "Waffles it is."

"Yes! Maple bacon waffles?" He threw a charming smile her way.

She nodded and he squealed in delight. A moment later, he raced down the hall, his feet pounded down the stairs. He was probably headed straight for the kitchen so that he could set out the ingredients.

Helper was Preston's middle name. Granted, he had a heavy hand with spices, but in waffles, that wasn't a bad element.

Dee grabbed her pale blue robe, draped over the foot of the bed, and wrapped it around her to ward off the chill. Her mother was going through "the change" and had the air conditioner set to the mid-sixties.

It felt like fall nipped at the door instead of summer. Delaney was more of a seventy-five or higher kind of girl.

Yawning, she trudged down the stairs and entered the kitchen. Sure enough, Preston had laid out all the items necessary and was waiting patiently. "Wash your hands."

He wiggled his fingers in the air. "Done."

"Okay, grab some flour."

Preston enthusiastically added ingredients to the batter. Once it was mixed, she poured it into the waffle iron. The smell of the waffles began to permeate the air, waking her better than a pot of coffee.

Once they were done, she placed two waffles in front of him.

"Thanks, Mom."

"Welcome."

She turned to refill the waffle iron. It was probably her favorite appliance in the kitchen. The waffles were always nice and thick, with deep pockets warm and ready for the syrup.

In spite of their abundant fluffiness, Preston could still pack them away. Once Philip was up, she'd need to make more to fill their tummies.

"Morning," Philip called as he entered the kitchen. His curly black hair was tousled every which way.

"Morning, Philip. Hungry?"

He nodded sleepily. Her mother breezed in, wearing standard work wear for The Maple Pit: jeans and a t-shirt.

"Morning, guys," Mrs. Williams said.

"Morning, Ma." Delaney held a plate piled high with waffles. "Waffles?"

Her mother shook her head. "I need to head in and show Luke how to do food prep for breakfast."

"He's working for breakfast?" Her stomach flopped, an image of him with the chef's double-breasted jacket flashed in her mind. She thought his height would make him appear awkward but assurance had oozed from him during last night's dinner rush. How could a man that ruggedly handsome cook so well? It was a dichotomy she was tempted to explore.

Ignore his good looks, Dee, and remember his day job.

Her heart squeezed. Luke was on leave. When it was over, he'd be back on some army fort working for Uncle Sam, while she remained in Maple Run. She ignored the twinge of emotion that flittered through her.

No time to examine it.

"Yes, I figured he needed to learn all the mealtimes so we can rotate and not burn out."

"Do you have any idea when Dwight will be back at work?"

"He has to wear the cast for six weeks." Sadness tinged her mother's voice.

"What?" Her mouth dropped open. "Luke's only going to be here for three and a half more weeks." Which was way too long in her opinion.

"I know. We talked about it briefly last night. I'm going to see if Nina can hire a temporary replacement by the time Luke leaves."

"So he's staying." It was more statement than question.

"He is." Her mother eyed her. "Is there a problem?"

Dee shook her head. No way did she wanted her mother in her head and exploring her feelings on the subject of Luke Robinson. Her mother was a fan of talking about everything. Delaney shuddered.

Feelings were supposed to be stuffed so far down you couldn't find them if you tried. Of course, she didn't think that way about every feeling, but when it came to the opposite sex it was a completely different matter.

Particularly, when it came to a certain Texan with ice blue eyes. One who made her think about dating and fairytale endings.

Not going to happen, Delaney. Remember what he does for a living.

God help her if she ever forgot.

Chapter Seven

Breakfast time.

It was Luke's favorite part of the day. Nothing like a big spread of protein and a pot of coffee to fuel one's day. Adding maple to the ingredients seemed like a stroke of genius.

He'd always thought the concoction a little too bland but the dark amber used in their waffles and pancakes was nothing short of amazing. He'd be a maple convert for life.

Apparently, the Williams family tapped the maple trees on their property. Mrs. Williams had shared their family tradition and all it entailed.

Unfortunately, the trees didn't produce enough to keep the restaurant in supply throughout the year. So they purchased maple syrup from a family-owned business in Vermont and other maple retailers.

It had been an enlightening conversation. Mrs. Williams practically sparkled with excitement as she relayed the process.

He peeked at her as she readied an order. Once she hit her cooking groove, she was actually pretty quiet. He thought he would have the morning off, but she wanted to show him the morning routine.

Part of him wanted to ask how Delaney was, but he didn't want to be too obvious. He plated the waffles that were topped with bits of maple-flavored bacon, despite having bacon baked into the batter as well. *Could you ever really have too much bacon?*

"It's funny you just made that." Mrs. Williams smiled at him. "Delaney was making waffles this morning."

Just the opening he needed. "How is she?"

"Looked half alive this morning." She chuckled. "I'm sure Preston dragged her out of bed. She likes to sleep in."

So did he.

"Is she off today?" He tried to infuse a nonchalant tone into his voice, but he must have failed.

Mrs. Williams stilled and looked him straight in the eyes. "She is," she replied slowly. "Is there something you need to tell me, Luke Robinson?"

He gulped. She sounded just like his Gram. "No, ma'am."

Mrs. Williams turned and reached for some bananas. "You know...Parker's been gone for a few years."

"I know." *Three to be exact.*

"Mm-hmm. I've always thought my daughter too good to just waste away until the Lord sees fit to carry her home. I mean she's only in her thirties. She could remarry and have a long successful marriage."

He tugged at his collar. "I'm sure she could."

"I just can't seem to convince her to start dating again. She needs to get her feet wet, if you get my drift."

He nodded.

"Plus, Maple Run is lacking in the interested-and-available pool of men."

"Small towns are like that at times."

"I agree." She looked at him again. "Although now I'm beginning to wonder if it wasn't part of God's timing. Seems like someone could catch her eye if he wanted to."

He blinked. Was she giving him the green light? A spark of hope lit inside him. If a man could get the approval of a woman's parents, then all the rest was a piece of cake. "Maybe he's not sure she'll go for it, considering his line of work."

She nodded. "There is that. But what harm is there in dating and seeing what happens? Of course, a fella could do the smart thing and leave that part up to God. Just express his interests and let the rest happen as it's supposed to."

His heart pounded in his chest. Expressing his interest was what kept him awake most of the night. Could he do it? Just walk up and tell her he liked her? Something so juvenile but so complex all at the same time.

"Don't be scared, Luke. God's got you."

With a wink, she went back to cooking in silence.

With last night's conversation with Micah and this morning's conversation with Delaney's mother, Luke began to think God was trying to tell him something. For sure the feelings he experienced whenever Delaney was near him were ones he needed to pray away.

After all, how could you atone for sins when you were mooning over the woman you inadvertently wronged? Yet now, he was wondering if God wasn't offering him an opportunity to find love.

Lord, do you really want me to tell Delaney I like her? He wiped a hand down his face and rested his elbows on his knees. The park was bright and sunny today, birds and cicadas added to the cacophony of noise.

Yet, the sounds of summer did nothing to soothe his soul. His insides felt more twisted up than a tangled fishing line.

I like her, Lord. Really like her. I would love the chance to get to know her better and see if something could develop. But she's Jones's wife, and I'm supposed to go back to the military in three weeks.

Three weeks.

Could he try and start a relationship and then hightail it back to work? Sure, he would want to try and make a long-distance relationship work, but they rarely did.

Especially, in the military. He didn't know what he would do if he got a "Dear John" letter from her.

But could he leave in three weeks without letting her know how he felt? Wouldn't that be worse…wondering what if? If he didn't tell her, he might have always wondered what could have been. He groaned.

You have to tell her, Robinson.

If she rejected him, he'd suck it up like a man…like a soldier. What other choice did he have?

A child's yell broke through the silence. He turned and froze as he saw Delaney following two boys, who raced full speed ahead toward the jungle gym. Looked like she found something for her kids to do today.

Indecision kept him rooted on the park bench. Just because he saw her didn't mean he'd have to go over and say hello. Besides, she hadn't seen him.

As if she heard his thoughts, she turned and looked in his direction. She stopped abruptly and gave a small wave.

Great, now what? He waved in return but made no move to get up. He couldn't. It was one thing to admit his interest in Delaney. Another to voice his feelings aloud. He was a moron if he thought this would be easy.

Man up, Robinson.

Before he could change his mind, he forced his feet to walk in her direction. Delaney must have had a similar thought because she met him half way.

"Luke," she breathed out. "How are you?"

"Good. Just enjoying the sunshine."

She squinted up at him. "It's hot...and humid."

"I know." He laughed as her nose wrinkled. "I like being warm more than I do cold."

"This warm?"

Granted the heat had kicked up a notch but that could have been her presence and not the abundant sunshine. "I admit the humidity is a little daunting, but I needed to think, and the park is a good thinking place."

"I see." She blinked. "Oh, hey, let me introduce my boys."

They were over by the playground and out of earshot. She slipped her pinkies in her mouth and a whistle rent through the air.

His jaw dropped in amazement and his hand clutched the space above his heart. "Who taught you how to whistle like that?"

She ducked her head but not before he saw her rosy cheeks. "My dad." She shrugged. "I was always competing with Dwight, so I learned how to whistle. He still can't figure it out."

Neither could he, but he wasn't going to admit that right now. "Wow."

Her boys slowed down from their full out run as they made it to her side.

"Preston, Philip, I want you to meet Mr. Robinson." She laid a hand on each of them when she said their name. "He knew your daddy."

Their eyes widened. "Really?" The one in the red t-shirt asked.

That was Preston, right? "Yes, sir. It's a pleasure meeting you." Luke stuck out his hand.

Preston puffed his chest and shook his hand. "Nice to meet you, too." He tilted his head. "You talk funny."

"Preston," Delaney snapped out.

"It's okay. I'm from Texas."

Philip's mouth dropped open. "Can you ride a horse?"

"Sure can." He looked at Delaney, wondering if she remembered his offer of lessons.

"Cool," Philip whispered.

"What are you doing here in Virginia if you're from Texas?" Preston stared at him, his dark eyes full of curiosity.

"I wanted to meet your mom and tell her about your dad."

"She already knows about him. That's silly."

He laughed. What else could he say? He doubted Delaney wanted him to say he thought he was the reason their father died.

"Mr. Robinson knows more about what your dad did in the military."

"Are you in the Army?" Preston asked.

"I am." He felt Delaney stiffened beside him.

Oh, yeah, this was not going to be easy.

What had she been thinking? It was one thing to notice Luke—she snorted, how could she not? But to walk over and introduce her kids to him? Nothing short of insanity.

Now she was going to have to hear them ask questions about the military. Questions she was perfectly happy to avoid. Besides, if the subject of his job never came up, she could pretend that something could happen between them.

She blinked, shocked by the direction her thoughts took.

"What do you do?" Philip asked him.

Her boys were staring at him with wide-eyed curiosity. It would have been cute if her stomach wasn't busy rolling around in angst. The desire to get to know him better warred with self-preservation.

"I jump out of aircraft."

She shook her head. Never had she understood why anyone would jump out of a perfectly sound aircraft. Okay, so she knew there was a logical purpose behind it, but that didn't detract from the stupidity of it all.

Hearing him talk about his job gave her the reminder she needed. This was the reason to continue avoiding spending time with this soldier.

"Whoa," the boys said in unison.

Unease slithered down her spine. She needed to get the boys away before their admiration turned to hero worship...or worse.

Always running, Delaney.

She ignored the voice. "Well, we're headed to the playground area."

"Wanna come?" Preston asked.

No, no, no! Her body froze at the invite. Slowly, she met Luke's gaze. Once again, the ice blue eyes seemed to seek the secrets of her soul. Each look from his penetrating eyes pierced her heart. How much more could she take?

"Delaney?" he whispered.

The sound of her name on his lips was her undoing. No way it should sound so good. Despite her misgivings, she nodded.

A wide smile plastered on his face, grooves deepened around his mouth and disappeared into his beard. What would he look like with a clean-shaven face? Not that he needed to look more handsome than he already did.

Preston grabbed Luke's hand and dragged him toward the playground. She laughed in amusement, thankful someone else got to experience the power behind his tug. Philip followed alongside her sedately.

"Did Daddy do the same job, Mom?"

"He did."

"Did he die because he hit the ground?"

Nausea rose at the image. "No, sweetie. They wear parachutes." She paused. The boys had never asked for details. How could she tell him someone aimed an RPG at their helicopter to kill them? None of them had the option of jumping out first.

"Oh. Dad and Mr. Robinson jumped out of the same plane?"

Not the day he died! She sighed. "I'm not sure." Didn't Luke say Parker took his spot? She wasn't sure how that translated but Philip didn't really need to know all the minute details.

"How come he's not working now?"

"He's on vacation."

"Oh. Okay." He ran off and headed for the slides at top speed.

She sighed in relief, thankful his questioning was complete. Luke walked towards her and her stomach dipped. *Out of the frying pan and into the fire.*

"How's your day been?" Luke's low timbre seemed to meld into the air.

"Pretty good despite my rude awakening." At his look of curiosity, she explained how Preston woke her up.

He laughed, the corners of his eyes crinkling. "Hey, a boy's gotta eat."

"You sound like him," she shook her head. "I didn't mind too much. I haven't slept in since they were born. For some reason they like to get up with the sun. Well, Pres does anyway. Philip just follows his stomach."

"Sounds like Preston doesn't want to miss anything."

"It's true. He has a million questions usually. It's interesting seeing life from his viewpoint."

"Do they like school?"

"Yes, thankfully. They make good grades."

"Awesome."

She turned to him. "What about you? Did you like school?"

"Loved it. For the longest time, I thought I would become a doctor or something that would allow me to use my love for science."

"Why didn't you?"

"Good old-fashioned burnout. Didn't want to go to college straight away. My father let me know freeloaders weren't welcome in his home, so I joined the Army."

He must have seen the stunned surprise on her face because he held a hand up. "My dad's not mean...just a strong advocate in people contributing back to society and kids leaving the house at eighteen."

"I get that. My dad was the same." She smiled thinking about the robust man. Sometimes she couldn't believe he was no longer living. *Why do you take people away, Lord?*

"What about you?" Luke took a step closer, standing right next to her. "Did you like school?"

"No," she said with a laugh. "I hated it. The only time I had fun was in English class."

"Was it the reading or writing?"

"Definitely the reading. I could spend the whole day reading if I had the opportunity."

"What's your favorite book?"

She studied him, wondering why the twenty questions. Yet the question refused to leave her lips. "Gone with the Wind."

"Really?" His eyebrows rose in surprise. "Why?"

"Because as brave as Scarlett was, she was terrified to be with the guy she loved."

An echo of awareness trembled through her. Was she doing that with Luke? *Nonsense, you hardly know him.* Wasn't that her fault?

Here he was asking questions, getting to know her, and she wanted to run away as if he was an axe murderer, terrified that the more she knew about him, the more he would appeal to her on a deeper level.

He already had her senses reeling, she didn't want her heart to follow suit.

"I'm glad you said that."

"Why?" The sudden gleam in his eyes unnerved her. She took a step back, but it was no use. He quickly closed the gap right back.

"I have some experience with fear."

"What could you be afraid of?"

"Of letting the woman I'm interested in know how I feel. I'm scared she'll dismiss my feelings and ignore her own."

Finding Love

Her mouth went dry at his implications. *He liked her?* Her insides screamed like an adolescent. A thrill of excitement shot through her. Luke liked her. She met his gaze, loving the look of interest on his face.

"If I tell her, would she go out with me?"

She licked her lips. Would she? Her circumstances hadn't changed. His job *hadn't* changed. But her desire to get to know him and see if there were any sparks was slowly rising.

"She might."

"Hmm, then I guess I'll wait until she's certain."

He stepped back and turned to watch the boys play.

What on earth just happened?

Chapter Eight

Luke couldn't believe he chickened out.

Instead of asking Delaney out right and proper, he hinted and evaded. *Smooth, Robinson, real smooth.* He wanted to punch himself in the face, but made excuses for his behavior.

It's not like she gave an emphatic yes anyway. Just a "might." And really, what did that mean? Sounded like she could lean toward "no" and he wasn't asking her out just for her to reject him. So instead, he lobbed the ball in her court.

At least, that's what he told himself.

Only the look of shock on her face made him wonder if that was such a good move. Her milk-chocolate brown eyes had hinted at interest for the first time since they met at The Maple Pit.

Shouldn't that have been good enough to ask her out?

Except, he was really afraid of rejection.

Why?

"She matters, Lord," he whispered to himself.

Finding Love 73

Delaney Jones had snuck her way past his barriers. The ones he erected when his almost fiancée decided she didn't want to be with a soldier. His job wasn't good enough to keep her in the lifestyle she desired. It'd hurt at the time, but dumping him was the best thing Bianca could have done for him.

The inkling of feelings he experienced around Delaney felt stronger than the ones he had around Bianca. How was that possible? Wasn't it too soon to be attracted to someone so strongly?

Dizziness gripped him as his mind experienced a roller coaster of emotions. Up and down, loop around. It was unbelievable. What happened to his nothing box, where he could cheerfully rest in for the rest of his life?

Nothing to think about, just be, and relax. Who could he call for advice? It needed to be someone older and wiser and not ruled by their hormones. He pressed speed dial.

"Hello?" The gruff tone of his father's voice calmed him down.

"Hey, Pop. Do you have a minute?"

"Sure do, what's going on?"

Luke leaned back into the rocking chair on the back porch at Bella's B&B. A slight breeze blew in the evening sky.

"I need advice."

"Girl trouble?"

He grinned. "You know it."

"You know I've been out of the market for a while. I'm not rightly sure how I can help you."

"How soon is too soon to have deep feelings for another person? Well, not necessarily deep," he hedged. He ran a hand over his beard, "Just deeper than surface level."

"You interested in Delaney?"

His Pop always did cut to the chase. "Yes."

"Hmm, you're certainly in a quandary, aren't ya?"

"I am." He laughed at his Pop's word choice.

"Well, Son, have you prayed?"

"I have."

"Then leave the rest to God. You always did think too much. Take a breath and stop trying to worry yourself to death. If your feelings are going too fast, faster than God would like, He'll slow you down. The rod of correction is a mighty force."

"Ouch, Pop." He winced thinking about his heart *and* being corrected by the Almighty.

His father chuckled. "Better make sure your spiritual ears are tuned into Him, Son. He won't steer you the wrong way."

It was good advice. Not entirely what he was hoping his father would say, but how could he argue? "Thanks, Pop."

"Of course, what else is going on with you?"

He told his Pop how he was filling in as a temporary chef while Dwight healed. He overheard Mrs. Williams say they would still have to hire a chef. Delaney's brother would be in a cast for a minimum of six weeks.

The man was probably going crazy being away from the kitchen and regulated to home. Then again, Dwight made sure to visit his wife at The Pit, so he wasn't completely isolated to home.

"Sounds like life's been pretty busy for you."

"In a good way."

"I'm glad. Now maybe you'll see there's more to life than the military."

He squeezed his eyes shut. "I know that, Pop. But I also have two years left to retirement. That's a nice check I could collect until I die."

"Money's not everything, Son."

Luke tried to stifle a sigh. He knew it wasn't, but it would be nice not to have to worry about it as well. A retirement check would pretty much eradicate the worry factor. "I'm still praying about it, Pop."

"Glad to hear it. You call me before you head back down here, all right?"

"Will do. Tell Grams I'll call her soon."

He hung up and stared out at the landscape. His Pop was right. He couldn't worry about whether or not Delaney was going to make a move.

Probably shouldn't even worry about money and whether it would ease his life after the military. The only thing he was certain of was that God would still be God regardless of his choices.

But it was high time he thought of a plan for life after the military, regardless if he reenlisted. He'd had sense enough to get a degree, but still that didn't always easily translate to a job outside of the military.

Some of his buddies knew exactly what they would do when they got out. He had a vague idea of returning to Texas and working on his father's land. Micah had suggested he do something with motorcycles since he was such an enthusiast.

Yet his dreams didn't sound like marketable or profitable occupations. Could he support a wife and kids without the aid of a military retirement check?

Whoa.

Where did that thought come from? He needed to go out with a woman before he started thinking about marriage, didn't he?

Lord, my thoughts are reeling. Spinning out of control. Please help me keep my eyes focused on the right issue: You. Please guide my decision on reenlisting. Also, I need a life plan for after my enlistment, whether I retire or not. What do I do with my life? And how do I handle my feelings for Delaney?

His feelings were all over the map. From wanting to maintain his distance, to wanting to be closer. Spending time with her and her boys at the park was nice. They seemed like good kids and his normal nervous behavior around kids was suspiciously absent.

Are You trying to tell me something?

"Guess I don't have to figure out everything tonight, Lord."

Remembering he left his prayer unfinished, he added a soft "Amen."

"Mama, someone's at the door."

Delaney blinked in confusion. She hadn't heard the doorbell ring. "Thanks, Pres. I'll get it."

He grinned, showcasing the gap where his two front teeth had been. She paused a moment, wondering why his missing front teeth bothered her.

When the thought failed to solidify, she ruffled his hair and headed for the front door. She slowed as she saw a silhouette through the glass pane to the right of the door.

Something about the layout of the house niggled in the back of her brain. Her mother's house didn't look like that.

"Who on earth?" she murmured. Going up on her tiptoes, she looked through the peephole.

Two Army officers stood on the porch in their dress uniform.

Parker.

Her mouth began to water and beads of perspiration popped across her forehead. Her hand shook as she reached for the door. Officers in their dress uniform was a bad sign.

Very bad.

She fumbled for the doorknob as tears blurred her vision.

Slowly, the door opened. Chaplain Franklin and Major Rhodes stood on her doorstep. She knew them. Had celebrated holidays with them because they worked with her husband.

She was dreaming. The thought was intense but didn't stop the dream from continuing.

"Can we come in Delaney?"

She shook her head vigorously, and wrapped her arms around her waist. "Where is he?"

"Delaney," Chaplain Franklin stated. "Let's go sit down in the living room."

The chaplain slowly entered the foyer, guiding her by the elbow toward her living room. They knew her home. She hosted a few parties for the soldiers to help encourage camaraderie and fellowship, as Parker always called it.

Chaplain Franklin sat next to her on her beige, floral patterned sofa as Major Rhodes squatted in front of her. Funny, the details one remembered. Her hands shook and goosebumps raced up her arms.

The air conditioner was set to seventy-seven. There was no reason for her to be cold, but a chill wrapped its way around her bones.

"Delaney," the Major began. He cleared his throat then met her gaze head on. "I'm sorry to inform you, but Parker's helicopter was shot down. There were no survivors."

The words could not have been any more devastating than if God Himself sent a messenger to inform her. It was like she'd lost the ability to take in any air.

All at once, the air left her body and a denial rose to her lips, falling like a benediction asking God for the Major to be wrong.

But he wasn't.

Delaney's eyes flew open as the remnants of the dream clung to her. Tears ran down her face and dampened her pillow. She glanced at the clock…*midnight*.

Of all nights to have the dream, it had to be after Luke hinted at a relationship.

She sighed, sitting up in the middle of her bed. Once upon a time, she'd only stick to the right side of the bed. After Parker's death, she filled the bed with dozens of throw pillows to prevent the loneliness.

Bits of her past warred with her present.

An image of the folded flag she received on behalf of the Army scrolled through her mind. She remembered clinging to it as tears streamed down her face.

The overbearing smell of dirt and rain. The sound of "Taps" crying out into the air as the bittersweet notes left the bugle.

The boys had clung to her side and would for the next month before the pain of their father's passing eased into something that was more functional.

Somehow, the three of them had found their rhythm again. Moving back to Maple Run had certainly helped.

Delaney sniffed. Was she insane for imagining she could date Luke? For a brief moment, she'd felt pure bliss at his interest. Her mind hadn't thought of Parker, of her widowhood.

No, it had been purely focused on Luke's ice blue eyes. Of the scent of Irish Spring wrapping around her in the summer breeze.

No, there was no way she could date another man who'd choose to put on a uniform and fight for his country. It was a noble occupation, but she wanted no part of it.

Then what are you going to tell Luke?

He wasn't her worry. Self-preservation had gotten her this far. It would take her further. Making the decision to date after losing a husband wasn't as big a concern as dating another solider.

A shudder shook her body, adding a chill to her already cold room. Why did she have to be interested in Luke?

Can't you take these feelings away, Lord?

Early on in her marriage, she and Parker had a discussion about what happened if the other should die. Being an Army soldier that deployed to hostile countries raised Parker's probability.

Not one she thought would come true, but it was there. They agreed the other should marry without worry of tarnishing the other's memory. She'd want Parker to marry if he had been the one still alive.

The past few years though, remarrying hadn't even entered her hemisphere of thoughts. Not even dating. However, one gaze from a rugged, heart-stopping Texan and she was quaking in her proverbial boots.

Not because he wasn't Parker but because of his uniform. Who knew she would be attracted to another soldier? She'd curse her hormones if she thought it would do any good.

With a whimper, she flopped back onto her pillows. Staying up and contemplating life's answers wasn't going to make her change her mind. Luke Robinson was in the military.

A soldier in the United States Army to be exact.

Off limits.

"You got that, Delaney? He's off limits."

Somehow, she had a feeling her heart wouldn't listen.

"Lord, please," she whispered in the quiet of her bedroom. "Please make sure my heart listens. I can't be with him. I just can't. Besides, You wouldn't ask that of me, would You?"

That was beyond irony, wasn't it?

Chapter Nine

Luke whistled softly as he plated the dinner order. Monday had a nice rhythm to it. It wasn't as slow as he thought it would be but not so fast-paced it would incite panic.

The Maple Run locals, mostly families, were enjoying dinner. The atmosphere in the kitchen was laid back as the soft strands of contemporary Christian music filled the air, mingling in with sounds of laughter from the dining area.

Life was good.

Except for the number of times he'd lost focus and stared at Delaney as she made her way from the tables to the kitchen to turn in the patrons' orders.

Each time she neared the service window his pulse skittered into a frantic cadence of attraction. At first, she avoided him as if a stench of a skunk clung to his skin.

As the evening headed toward night, however, she began to meet his gaze.

He swallowed as she headed his way again. Her table's order was ready. Could he get a smile out of her? Anything to give him a glimpse of hope? She slowed as she neared the window.

"Order's up," he stated.

"Thanks." She began to grab the plates, all without making eye contact.

Two steps forward, three steps back. "Delaney?"

"Hmm?" She paused, her eyes focused on the plates.

"You look mighty pretty." He licked his lips, wondering if he sounded as foolish as he felt.

Her gaze flew upward and met his. Her lips curved into a heart stopping grin. "Thank you, Luke." She turned away and melted into the crowd.

Victory came fast and sweet.

That beauty of a smile was worth feeling a little foolish. Luke whistled as he finished a couple of more orders then took off the apron and placed it on a hook. He tapped on Alex's back, who then slipped his headphones off.

"I'm heading to break."

"All right, man." Alex raised an eyebrow. "Why don't you just ask her out instead of stalking her with your eyes?"

His neck warmed under the younger man's scrutiny. "I have my reasons."

"Pathetic." Alex shook his head.

Luke whirled around and headed for the breakroom. He didn't want to see the look of pity on Alex's face.

There was nothing he could do about his earlier mistake. If he asked her out now, wouldn't she wonder why he didn't do it before?

He grunted and ran a hand down the back of his head. Dating was for the birds. It was exhausting, and all he'd done was think about it.

Maybe if he came up with an action plan the desperation clawing at his gut would back down to a simple gnawing of the bone.

The breakroom was silent, and he sighed in relief. No one would be around if his ruminations turned to mumbling under his breath. He wasn't always aware of his actions while his mind came up with a plan. It was a wonder his military call sign wasn't Mumbles instead of Crusoe.

As he ate bits of his meatloaf, his mind worked through different scenarios. He could walk Delaney to her car after work and ask her out.

Maybe equate her beauty to the moon and once she smiled at the compliment, ask her out.

He shook his head. Too lame.

What about casual like? He could ask her when she dropped off a food order. Alex would have his headphones on, so hopefully he wouldn't hear him stumble over the question.

Then again, if she rejected him, it was always possible someone would overhear.

Nah, that wouldn't work.

Just as he took a bite of his macaroni and cheese, the breakroom door opened. Delaney strolled in with a hot plate of food.

"Hi, Luke."

He nodded dumbly.

She stared at the table looking to the seat next to him and the one across from him. He straightened up in his chair. *What was she thinking?* She took an audible breath and headed for the seat across from him.

"How's the meatloaf?" She pointed to his plate.

He swallowed the food in his mouth in a hurry to answer. "Good."

"That's nice." She gave him a tight-lipped smile.

This conversation was painful. It gave a whole new meaning to "walking on eggshells." If this is what people meant, he didn't ever want to do it again.

"Delaney—"

"Luke—"

"You first," he motioned with his hand.

"I had a horrible dream last night."

Concern tightened his gut. "Are you all right?"

She shook her head, her ponytail swinging. "No," she whispered. "I wasn't even planning on telling you that."

He reached for her hand and stopped. Would she welcome a hand to hold for comfort? He placed his hand on the table, inches from hers. "Do you want to talk about it?"

"Not really, but I do need to talk."

"I'm listening." He placed his fork down and gave her his undivided attention.

"Your job scares me. I was married to a man who had your job. I know what you do, well as much as you can say." She waved a hand in the air. "What I'm trying to say is…" she broke off and stared at her plate, various emotions crossing her face.

"You're worried I'll get hurt." He didn't say "die," although his mind practically shouted it.

She nodded, and a tear slipped down her cheek.

He closed his eyes. "I'm sorry," he whispered. He'd been so foolish to think he'd have a chance with her.

How could he ask her to date him when her husband died from job hazards?

His eyes flew open at the touch of her hand.

"Don't be."

He stared at their hands. The contrast in shades tugged at his heart, evidence of their differences.

It wasn't about their skin color, but somehow it was a reminder that they came from two different paths in their life. She a widow, he a single man. He wrapped his hand around hers, the warmth curling around his heart.

Why did he have to let her go?

"About what I said at the park..."

"Yes?"

Was it his imagination or was her voice slightly breathless? He inhaled trying to draw strength. If she was scared to make the next step because of his job, then he owed it to her to back away.

"Forget it."

"What? Why?" She pulled her hand away as confusion filled her face.

"You just said you were scared because I have the same job as Jones."

"So..."

Now it was his turn to feel confused. "But..."

She held a hand up. "I didn't tell you that so you would go running the opposite direction," she snapped.

"Hold on." He reached for her hand, but she scooted her chair back. "What are you trying to tell me then?"

"Forget it." She headed toward the door, her dinner an afterthought.

"Delaney." He hopped out of his seat and slid in front of the door before she could reach it. "Delaney," he whispered. He cupped her shoulders, marveling at her height.

It allowed him to look right into her chocolaty brown eyes. "I like you...a lot...but I don't want to cause you any more turmoil than I already have. When you said you were scared, I was trying to do the right thing and back away."

"No one asked you to," she whispered.

"Then what do you want me to do?"

"Go out with me," she blurted out.

A glimmer of heat filled his insides. "Yes."

She blinked as if stunned. Whether it was by her question or his response remained to be seen. Slowly, he slid his hands down her arms and intertwined his fingers with hers. "I'd love to go out with you."

"Okay." She blinked again. "I'm off Thursday."

"Thursday it is."

He couldn't remember if he had that day off, but he'd do everything in his power to ensure he did.

Delaney knocked on Nina's office door. Her heart was galloping like a stallion. She couldn't believe what just happened. She'd been intent on steering clear of Luke, but somehow she'd ended up asking him out.

"Come in."

She opened the door thankful to see no other employees in her sister-in-law's office. Just the woman herself. Her white desk was immaculate except for a couple of white picture frames.

Probably held Dwight and the kids' picture.

"Hey, Dee, what's up?" Nina leaned back in her white leather chair.

"Can you talk?"

Nina arched an eyebrow skyward. "Sure. What's wrong?"

"I just asked Luke out." She flopped into the seat adjacent Nina's desk.

"Really?" Nina leaned back with a small smile edging her lips.

"Yes," she cried out. "I didn't mean to." She really hadn't. Yet, each time she picked up an order or dropped one off, the Texan's blue eyes had tugged at her heart. Then he had to go and tell her she looked pretty.

No, mighty pretty. It had sounded like a line straight from a western romance. He'd given her no choice but to seek him out.

"I take it asking him out's a bad thing?"

"Of course it is! He's in the Army for heaven's sake! The Army!" She stood up and clutched the back of her vacant seat. "I wanted to tell him it wouldn't work. The next thing I know I'm telling him I'm scared. Scared! It's mortifying what that man does to me when I get too close. One look at his eyes and my insides liquefied. Then, I asked him out." She snorted in disgust.

"I don't see what the problem is."

She squinted her eyes at Nina. It was obvious her sister-in-law was holding back laughter. "What in the world is so funny? My life's in shambles and you're suppressing giggles."

"Oh, Dee, calm down. You're attracted to a man. You aren't the first widow to give another man a second glance."

"I wish it was only two glances," she muttered.

This time Nina's laugh bounced in the office. She shook her head at the woman's antics.

"I bet you sounded angry when you asked him out."

Delaney's lips twitched. Then a smile broke out. "Probably."

Nina clutched the side of her stomach as laughter racked her body. "Oh, my goodness. I would have loved to been a fly on *that* wall."

"Nina," she sighed. She sat back down. "What am I going to do? Seriously, I can't date him. He's on vacation and will go back home soon. Back to the Army and a life of jumping out of moving aircraft." She enunciated each word slowly as disbelief coursed through her. "I don't know if I can handle that."

"No one says you have to marry him. Just date. Have fun. Give yourself an opportunity to relax and unwind with an adult."

She bit her lip. It *had* been awhile since she had an adult to talk to that wasn't related to her. And their conversations in the past were intriguing.

Maybe she could have fun and not make a big deal out of it. "You're right. It's just one date."

"Exactly. No one's proposing." Nina paused. "Wait, you didn't secretly place an ad in the paper, did you?"

Delaney chuckled. "No, only you're crazy enough to do that."

Nina smiled sheepishly. "It worked out though." She paused. "When are you two going out?"

"Thursday," she squeaked.

"Where's he taking you? What are you going to wear?"

Panic clawed at Delaney. "I don't know. Clothes."

Nina's mouth dropped open. "Of course you're wearing clothes, Delaney. But it has to be the *right* ones."

"Didn't you just say it was just a date?" The woman was confusing her.

"Sure, it is. You still want to look your best though. Think of it as a test run for when you're ready to get back out there for marriage purposes."

She shuddered. Shopping had never been her favorite activity. In fact, she hadn't gone shopping in about…three years. *Wow!*

"Don't panic." Nina's voice was calm. "I'll help you. We could go shopping earlier that day and make it a ladies' day. What do you think?"

For the first time, calm found her. "That sounds great, Nina." She didn't have many opportunities to hang out with her sister-in-law. She always felt like she had to make up for their rocky start.

"Perfect," Nina beamed.

The rest of her shift, Delaney tried to calm herself. It was only one date. Certainly that wasn't enough time to actually fall for a guy.

When Luke's vacation was over, she wanted to be able to say good-bye and thank him for his friendship. She wouldn't do it if she ended up falling for him.

Despite the calm assurance Nina had offered, panic edged its way back in.

Lord, I'm begging you here. Please don't let me fall for this man. Help me to view this date as a stepping stone to enter the dating scene again. Nothing serious, just one date.

One date.

She could do it. Wear something nice, remember the wit and charm she'd used once upon a time for something other than greeting customers at The Pit.

Laugh at a man's jokes and go through the twenty questions trying to decide if they were compatible.

Her stomach rolled. Scratch that. This wasn't an interview for a life partner. Just two people getting together to pass the time. It didn't matter if she was compatible with Luke.

Didn't even matter if there was a spark of attraction. *More like a flame.*

Her face heated. Okay she'd need a lot more prayer to make sure her heart was safeguarded. No need to go out on a date unarmored.

Don't forget about me, Lord. I hope You're hearing all this. Seeing all this. I need a safety net a mile wide and high. Deep, too.

Chapter Ten

Luke leaned back in his chair, full and satisfied. Between eating at The Pit and the food Ms. Bella fed him, he'd definitely need to work off the extra weight before his leave was over.

She made pasta—gnocchi, she called it—from potatoes. It was the best pasta he'd ever eaten. In fact, all the food she cooked was amazing and inspired him to add Italy to his bucket list of places to visit.

The sound of the doorbell pealed through the air.

Ms. Bella rubbed her hands together. "New guest. I'll be back." Her skirt swished as she left the kitchen and headed for the front door.

Since he'd been here, one or two guests had always occupied the premises. However, he'd been the last one for the past three days.

It was kind of nice to get doted on, even though he felt bad for making Ms. Bella work for one person. Hopefully the new person would stay awhile and take some of the pressure off of him.

Then again, it was easier to help one than two.

"Come meet the other guest," he heard Ms. Bella say. She walked into the kitchen.

"Soup?" Luke stood to his feet and crossed the room. He slapped his best friend's back. "What in the world are you doing here?"

"Couldn't pass a chance to see you before you head back, especially since you're so close."

"You two know each other?" Ms. Bella arched an eyebrow, her finger pointing back and forth between them.

"Yes, ma'am," they said in unison.

The B&B owner chuckled. "Oh, good. You help your friend," she said to Micah. "He has the girl troubles."

"We're going out tomorrow, Ms. Bella, so things are looking up." He walked back to the table and motioned for Soup to sit. "Seriously, man, what are you doing here?"

"Job interview."

"What? Where? For what?"

Micah sat back, crossing his feet at the ankles. "I got my Physician Assistant license so I'm looking for a job where I can use it. I'm interviewing with the local family practice."

"Nice. I forgot you went back to school for that."

"Yeah, it was brutal but worth it."

"Is this your only interview?"

"No, I have a couple of other ones, too. We'll see how they pan out." Micah sat forward, tapping his hands on the tabletop. "So, you and Delaney, huh? You finally manned up?"

Luke couldn't stop the grin that formed across his face. "She asked me out after I put the ball in her court." He shrugged. "Oddly enough it worked."

"Awesome. Maybe I could meet her before I have to go back home?"

"Dude, we haven't even been on a date. I don't want to give her a weird vibe about meeting my friends."

Micah rolled his eyes skyward toward his bald head. "You're worse than a girl sometimes."

"I don't think so," he said with a grin.

"I'm surprised you're eating here. I thought you ate at The Pit."

"Somedays I do and sometimes I eat here. Ms. Bella is an amazing cook. You should grab you a bowl." He motioned toward the countertops. "She always makes more than enough."

"She won't mind?"

"Nah."

Micah looked around. "Are you sure? Should I ask?"

"Just eat. She always leaves after she's done cooking. Doesn't want to bother anyone while they eat. Kinda like a ninja the way she disappears sometimes."

Micah sat back down and took a heaping bite. His eyebrows shot up at the first taste.

"Good, huh?"

He nodded his head, then visibly swallowed. "That's amazing."

"I may never want to leave Maple Run with all this good food."

"Then stay."

"And do what?" He ran a hand over his beard. "I don't want to be a chef. It's a hobby, not something I want to do every day." He sighed.

Cooking full time drained him, but Delaney needed him so he would continue helping out.

"You think about the Guard? You can do work on the weekends and still work toward a retirement check."

"Hmm."

"What's your degree in again?"

"Business."

Micah nodded slowly as he chewed his food. "Those that can't do, teach."

"What?"

"I don't know...it's some famous saying. I think you should teach."

"Teach what? If I teach other soldiers, I'd have to reenlist. I'm talking about when I get out, man."

"I know. You could teach as a government contractor."

"Hmm..." He rubbed his beard. "I wonder if they have any jobs like that out here."

"You thinking of moving up here, Crusoe?" Micah watched him, curiously.

If a relationship between him and Delaney worked out...why not? "Maybe."

"Well, something to look into."

"That it is."

Delaney's hatred of shopping intensified as she dragged herself behind Nina. The insane woman dashed from clothes rack to clothes rack, muttering underneath her breath.

As soon as they had stepped into the department store, her sister-in-law's sweet expression faded, replaced by her game face. She watched in bemusement as Nina darted toward another rack.

How the girl managed to grab a specific item from each rack without thumbing through all the offerings was enough to exhaust Delaney, but she admired Nina.

Nina stopped and turned to look at her. "Come on, girl! To the dressing room."

Oh, but she wanted to gripe! Why couldn't she just wear what was in her closet? This was a test run, not a real live date that would put stars in her eyes and have her writing Luke's name a thousand times on a piece of paper.

"Delaney, you're moving slower than a snail on a sloth."

She chortled. "Where in the world did that come from?"

"You hear strange things when you sit down and eat at The Maple Pit."

"Maybe you should write a book about it." She followed Nina into a dressing room. "Wait, you're not going to stay in here are you?"

"Of course not. I'm just hanging these up." Nina arched an eyebrow. "And don't think for a single minute that you can skip an outfit and not come out and show me."

"Yay." The words fell flat, her sarcasm shining through.

"Cheer up, sunshine. Once you try on the right outfit, your mood will improve dramatically."

Nina turned away but not before Delaney saw a glint of disappointment in her eyes. "Hey," she laid a hand on her sister-in-law's arm. "I'm sorry. I wanted to go shopping not because I like it but for us to become better friends."

"Really?" Nina searched her eyes, seeking truth.

You're an idiot. How could she forget how important family was to Nina?

The girl was willing to put herself out there and advertise for a husband for the sake of having a family of her own. And here she was complaining she had to go shopping when she willingly said yes.

Finding Love

"Really. I'm sorry I've been so grouchy."

"It's okay." Nina beamed. "Now go change."

Dee winced as she gazed in the mirror. The outfit was horrible. The shorts were way too short and the tank top didn't reach the waist band. She inhaled, sucking in the extra belly fat that stuck around way too long after her pregnancy.

She walked out into the waiting room and stared at the carpet, afraid to meet Nina's gaze.

"Oh, man, that's not at all what I imagined." Nina's eyes sparkled with laughter. "You can take that off now and end the torture."

"Thank God," she breathed out. Her little pouch poked over her waistband, and Nina fell over laughing.

"Yeah, yeah, don't act like you don't have one, too."

"Gotta love having twins, huh?"

"Definitely."

She wiggled out of the clothes and reached for the next outfit. A skirt and blouse, simple and hopefully the one.

The thought of going through the rest of the clothes and not finding the perfect date outfit was enough to make her hyperventilate.

Her mouth dropped open. She looked like a nun or...she wasn't sure what else to compare it to. *Nina should love this one.*

She did the cabbage-patch dance out the fitting room and into the waiting area.

"No, please don't do that or wear *that* ever again."

"Come on, I look stunning."

"You look like a school marm. You're missing your lunch pail."

"Hey, you picked it out."

"Yes, but it's not supposed to look like that." Nina shook her head. "It's much easier to shop for myself. It's because you're so tall."

"There is that." And Luke was taller than her.

"You thinking about Luke?"

Heat infused her face. "What do you mean?"

"I saw that look." Nina made a swirling motion toward her face. "You like him, like him, huh?"

"Maybe." She shrugged then ran for the safety of the fitting room. No need letting her sister-in-law entertain any grand ideas. This was a test date, just to see how she could do.

Not a love connection.

Next up was a maxi dress. It had three-quarter-length sleeves and fell to the floor. She twirled watching the bottom flare out. It was beautiful *and* comfortable. The yellow color seemed to deepen her skin tone to a rich brown.

"This is the one," she whispered.

She sauntered out the dressing room and struck a pose.

"Yes!" Nina shouted. "It's perfect. All you need are some accessories and you'll knock his socks off."

"Okay, I think I can handle that part. Necklaces aren't so bad."

"Don't forget earrings and shoes, maybe even a bracelet."

"Nina," she groaned out.

"No, sister dear, we're going to have fun. Besides, this wasn't so bad, was it?"

She smiled down at her petite friend. "It wasn't."

"Good. Luke Robinson won't know what hit him."

"I don't want to knock him out."

"Oh, yes, you do sweetie. I saw those moony eyes you were making."

She sighed. "But he's a soldier."

"And you have experience being a soldier's wife. Don't focus on the negative. When we do, we miss out on all the good God has for us."

"He's leaving."

"Then enjoy the view for however long it lasts."

"It is a spectacular view." Impressive stature, dark wavy hair, and dreamy blue eyes. Yes, the view was certainly spectacular.

"Moony eyes are back."

"Oh, hush." She tapped Nina on the arm as the younger woman guided them toward the shoe section.

"I'm just stating facts. Don't be mad. I'm sure I have a similar expression when I think about Dwight."

"Ugh, definitely. Both of you. I've never seen my brother so sappy."

Nina chuckled. "Then you haven't paid attention when he holds one of the twins."

"Probably because I'm doing the same thing when I hold them. They're so adorable. I swear I get baby fever every time I'm near them."

"Never too late—"

"Oh yes, it is," she interrupted. "That ship has sailed and sunk to the bottom of the ocean. No more kids for me."

"Really?"

"You want more?" She stared at her sister-in-law in disbelief. They had three kids. Granted, Kandi was eighteen and going to college soon, but still. "What if you got pregnant and had more twins?"

Nina grinned. "More to love."

"More power to ya, girl. My baby having days are over. O-v-e-r."

"I get it, I get it." Nina picked up a pair of heels. She shook her head no.

"What if Luke wants kids?" Nina grabbed a pair of wedged heels.

"Then he's not the one." Her gut sent a twinge of unease at the thought.

Could he want more kids? *Wait a minute.* They hadn't even had their date yet. No need to even go down this line of questioning. Besides, *if* he did and they were in a relationship, she'd just cross that bridge, and dive off to escape the inquiry.

"Don't discount it, Dee," Nina said in a sing-song voice.

"Already forgotten."

Chapter Eleven

The suspense just might kill him.

Luke glanced at his watch, doing quick math. He still had two hours to go before he could pick Delaney up for their date. Thankfully, he'd worked that morning at The Pit to help pass the time.

Well, really, he swapped shifts with Mrs. Williams so that he could go out with Delaney. It had been a little discomfiting…at least on his part. There had to be some rule about dating your boss's daughter and swapping shifts with them to ensure it happened.

Then again, Mrs. Williams gave her approval early on, so maybe he was just making everything difficult, like his Pop always said.

So convoluted.

His watch moved forward a minute. There really had to be something else he could do besides sitting on his bed and staring at the time. He ran a hand over his face and stilled. His fingers moved back and forth over his beard.

If he wanted to make the best of the date, he had to look his best.

Right?

Spurred by the thought, he headed for the on-suite bathroom. Somewhere in his toiletry bag was a razor. He always kept one in case he decided he wanted to shave. Or if the Army suddenly decided to call him back to work.

This much hair on his face went against regulations, so he was always prepared to rid himself of it. He pulled the razor out and stared at it. As much as he loved growing a beard on leave, it needed to go.

He grabbed his travel-size shaving cream and got to work. Eventually, the beard was gone and the lower half of his face stared back at him. It was lighter than the top half, but there was nothing he could do about that.

Guess he should have shaved it off yesterday and sat in the sun to help.

Luke glanced at his watch. *How was that only fifteen minutes?* He'd taken his time and gotten every single hair off his chin and neck. He didn't even nick himself. "Okay, God. That didn't take as long as I was hoping."

It was time to go with the flow because staring at his watch wouldn't speed up the minute hand. He would just get dressed and see what happened. Maybe Ms. Bella would want to shoot the breeze until he had to leave to pick up Delaney.

He smoothed down his blue plaid, button-down shirt. The rolled sleeves ensured he wouldn't melt going out in the summer heat. Then again, it was supposed to be a little cooler today.

Apparently the weather in Virginia was about as stable as horse on roller skates. A glance in the floor-length mirror assured him he looked presentable. He rubbed his smooth cheeks one more time.

Hopefully, Delaney liked the look. If not, he just wasted time for nothing. He grabbed his leather jacket and helmet. In a few steps, he reached the kitchen doorway where the smell of bread greeted him.

"Hi, Luke. You ready for your date?" Bella grinned, her eyes twinkling in merriment.

"Yes. A little nervous."

"Sure, sure. It is hard dating a single mother." Now that he met the boys, the single mom aspect didn't bother him so much. If only he could shake the memory of Jones. He winced. That sounded worse than he meant.

"You'll be fine. Delaney's a good person."

"That she is."

Bella sat his Harley Davidson saddlebag picnic basket on the kitchen island. "Your dinner's all ready."

"Thank you so much, Ms. Bella. I'm sure we'll enjoy it."

He grabbed the basket, thankful Ms. Bella offered to make their picnic dinner. Spending all day in the kitchen lessened his desire to cook. Plus, Delaney would get a chance to sample her wonderful cooking.

Luke stowed the picnic basket on his bike. He inhaled, trying to create an inner calm. No matter how many deep breaths he took, it did nothing to calm his nerves.

He muttered his life verse of John 14:27, "Peace I leave with you, my peace I give unto you: not as the world giveth, give I unto you. Let not your heart be troubled, neither let it be afraid."

Breathe, Robinson. It was now or never. Time to get Delaney for their date.

Their date.

"Bye, Ms. Bella."

"Have fun."

As he straddled his Roadster, a prayer rose on his lips. "Lord, be with me. Help me show her a good time. Help her relax and keep her fears at bay...and mine too."

His mind emptied as he became one with his Harley. *Left, right, straight.* He needed to stash the picnic basket before picking up Delaney. The peace of the ride flooded him, calming him.

The sun beamed down, heating his leather jacket. Thankfully, it didn't make him sweat. He'd come to appreciate the cool breeze that always seemed to hover in the Virginia air.

Especially since he'd be on a date in a matter of minutes.

After dropping the basket off, he drove down a road that led to a yellow farmhouse. The front porch had a few white rocking chairs. A couple of bikes and some sport balls littered the lawn.

All that was missing were the two kids they belonged to.

He gulped as he rolled to a stop. If he checked his watch, he knew fear would paralyze him. He was probably an hour early. Then again, maybe he should check it.

If he really was an hour early, Delaney would think him crazy. Of course, he could sit out here until it was exactly time for their date.

No. That had stalker written all over it.

"You can do this. Have fun. Show her a good time. Relax."

Then why did this feel scarier than jumping out of a helo?

He placed his helmet on the handlebar and headed for the porch. Sending up another short prayer, Luke knocked on the door. Tension rooted him to ground as the sound of footfalls reached his ears.

His breath whistled out his body as someone unlocked the door.

The door swung wide open and there stood Delaney in a light yellow dress that reached the floor. Her hair hung in dark waves against her shoulders. Her thick eyelashes seemed to emphasis the shape of her eyes.

His heart picked up speed and he gulped.

"Hi."

Whoa. Her brain officially short-circuited. She thought Luke was good-looking *with* his beard. Without it…well, words failed her. She couldn't look away. Her heartbeat picked up speed with such force she glanced down to make sure it wasn't visible.

Normal looking.

Her eyes swiveled back to his. They seemed to match the clear sky this afternoon. Her eyes dropped down to the part of his face that had been covered in the mountain-man style beard.

He was the most striking man she'd ever seen.

Saying "hi" seemed inadequate, but that was all her brain had been able to produce.

Her fingers itched to touch his cheeks as her mind wondered if they were as smooth as they looked. He must have sensed the emotions running through her, because a full-fledged grin broke across his face.

She gasped.

He has dimples!

Although, they were much too deep to be considered mere dimples. More like grooves of sexy goodness. She couldn't catch her breath.

"You are positively stunning." His Texas drawl lowered to baritone levels, sending shivers of awareness dancing up her bare arms.

"I need a sweater," she blurted out. She squeezed her eyes shut. "I mean, you look great as well."

He rocked back on his heels. "Thank you. I'll wait while you get it."

"Okay." She turned, closing her eyes in mortification. What was it about the man that had her mouth spilling all kind of secrets? She placed a hand over her heart. *What was I supposed to be doing?*

"Getting a sweater."

She jumped and whirled around, mortified that she had spoken the words out loud. "Oh, thank you." She raced up the stairs.

Her mother stood at the top of the stairs. "Well," she whispered. "What's he wearing?"

"It's not what he's wearing; it's what he's not."

"Excuse me?" Her mother leaned back, hand on hip.

She shook her head. "I meant he shaved. His beard is gone."

"And?"

"He has dimples." Her whispered tone took on an edge of panic. "How can I have a coherent conversation with a man with dimples?"

"What is it with you and Dwight and dimples?" Her mother shook her head. "Remember you have two boys, and I'm sure that'll bring you back down to earth."

Delaney blinked. Her mother was right. She was wigging out for nothing. "You're right. What was I thinking?" She took a deep breath and grabbed her navy cardigan. "See you, Ma."

"Have fun, sweetie."

Finding Love 105

It was foolish to have grabbed a sweater. It was summertime for crying out loud. Why hadn't she said purse? Now she'd be forced to carry the sweater or risk looking foolish. *More foolish than wearing a sweater in the summer?*

Her steps faltered as Luke came into view.

His face, sans beard, blinded her with the intensity of a morning sun, yet she couldn't look away. Her false bravado left the building. She squeezed the sweater, trying to dry her damp palms. Her pulse pounded in her ears.

"You ready?"

"Yes," she squeaked. She cleared her throat. "I'm ready."

"Great, this way."

He led her toward the side of the house where the driveway was located. She stopped short. "Where's your car?"

"Delaney," he said slowly. "You know I drive a motorcycle."

"I...somehow, I forgot." Even that sounded idiotic to her own ears. *How could she forget?*

He smirked. "I'm a good rider. You'll be safe."

"I have a dress on."

Luke slid a hand down the back of his neck. "Sorry. I really didn't think of that part."

"We could take my car."

He bit his lip, indecision darkening his eyes. "I kind of wanted to surprise you with the location."

"All right. You can drive." She snapped open her clutch and tossed him the keys to her relic. Normally, she didn't like anyone driving her car, but Luke...something about him was different.

Besides, if he put a dent in it, no one would notice.

Luke guided her toward the passenger side, his hand settled at the small of her back. Her skin heated up as the warmth of his hand seeped through the layers of her clothing.

Didn't he know she was already warm from the weather? There had to be a way to tone down his appeal.

He pulled the door open and smiled at her. "Can I just say one more time that you are absolutely breathtaking?"

Okay, so compliments would only make her insides liquefy further. "Thank you, Luke." Her eyes dropped to his lips. Lips which were no longer hiding behind hair.

She dropped into the passenger seat, unnerved by her thoughts. Wasn't this just supposed to be fun between friends? Who thought of kissing their friend?

Snap out of it, Delaney. She watched as Luke rounded the front of the car before opening the door.

Luke settled into the driver's seat, adjusting the mirrors. He started the car then stopped and looked at her. "I feel like there's some tension between us."

"Nerves." *Why did you admit that?*

A puff of air escaped his lips. "Good to know I'm not the only one."

"You're nervous?"

"Like you wouldn't believe. I don't think you realize how gorgeous you are. It's enough to make any man quake in his boots."

She chuckled. "Well, right back at ya. I can't get over the look without the beard. You were handsome before but…" She shook her hand as if to insinuate how hot he was.

"See, being honest isn't so bad, is it?"

"Terrifying."

He let out a bark of laughter. "Right?" He nudged her lightly with his elbow. "I just want us to be comfortable. You know...have fun."

Fun. It's what she'd been telling herself all along but failing miserably at. "Fun it is, Luke Robinson."

She offered her hand, to shake on the promise. Instead, Luke took it and placed a kiss on her palm. Every nerve stood at attention.

Whether it was from shock or the softness of his kiss, she wasn't sure. Her brain wasn't even able to form a coherent thought.

Oh, my. He was going to make fun mighty difficult.

Chapter Twelve

Luke held the oars above the water, allowing the current to carry them along the Potomac River. Delaney had a smile of pure delight stretched across her face, her arms wrapped around her knees. She'd been surprised when they arrived at the boating dock, but no less enthused.

Yesterday, he called ahead to make sure they had a rowboat available for rental. Thankfully, they did. A speedboat would have ruined his plans for a relaxing date.

"This is so peaceful, Luke."

"Isn't it?" He watched her as she tilted her head back, letting the sun's rays caress her face. Never had he been jealous of the sun before.

He dipped the oars in the river and paddled. They were nearing the picnic area. The owner of the boat rentals was fine with him staking claim on a picnic area. He'd already laid out the blanket.

Just needed to get the girl to the site.

At first, he'd considered horseback riding for a date, but he'd hesitated. His instincts told him to save it for a time when she could bring her boys along. Despite the fact that being around kids was slightly terrifying. *No.* It was more than that. They were Jones's kids. The need to prove himself worthy had increased exponentially with that knowledge.

Delaney leaned forward. "Don't laugh."

"Okay."

"I've never been on a boat before."

"Really? Maple Run is so beautiful. It has a lot to offer outdoors."

"True, but..." She shrugged. "I guess I'm a walking kind of girl. I've been hiking to some of the national parks, but get me in something other than a car, and I usually panic."

"How come you didn't panic today?"

"Too busy loving the romance of it all."

His heart dipped to his stomach. Romance was his aim, and apparently he'd hit the mark. "Are you always this honest?"

She laughed. "Hardly, but you seem to bring it out in me."

"Likewise." He winked, loving the way her cheeks took on a pink hue. His stomach interrupted the silence.

"Hungry, huh?" Laughter tinged Delaney's voice.

"Yes. Thank goodness we're here." He pointed behind her toward the dock, lined with trees. He could only imagine what it would look like in the fall or springtime.

As it was, the greenery added a coziness that was missing from west Texas scenery.

After he secured the boat, he held her hand as she climbed out. He laced his fingers through hers, rubbing his thumb along the back of her hand. He couldn't help but note the perfect fit.

He led her to the picnic area, where a checkered blanket lay spread out with the picnic basket resting on top.

"Wow," she murmured. She stopped and looked at him. "Thank you so much. This is wonderful."

"Anytime."

He knelt down and began pulling out the food Ms. Bella had prepared. Next came the patterned, disposable plates. Satisfied with the presentation, he started a playlist on his cell.

Delaney's eyebrows rose as the music filled the air. "You've thought of everything, huh?"

He shrugged, "Maybe." Okay, so he'd created the playlist last night. He figured the mix of Christian and Country music would help them relax, if not add to the romance factor.

"Smooth."

"Ha, not really. Remember the motorcycle?"

"Yeah, I can't believe you expected me to get on it in this dress." Her head shook in bemusement.

Heat filled his face. "Next time I'll remind you to wear jeans." *Except he liked the look of her in a dress.* It was a reminder to treat her like she deserved. Plus, she looked gorgeous in it.

"You expect me to ride that?" Her voice went up an octave, and her eyes widened.

"Let me guess, a panic trigger for you?"

"Definitely. Do you know what happens to people who ride motorcycles?"

"They get to point B a lot faster."

She shook her head. "I don't even know what to say to that."

"Let's ride?" He grinned.

Delaney ducked her head and mumbled something that sounded like "dimples." He didn't know whether to call her on it or take a bite of his sandwich. The sandwich won.

After he swallowed his bite, he took a gamble. "I promise I won't let anything happen to you. You'll love the ride." He held up the scout's pledge. "Scout's honor."

"I don't know." Her lips twisted in indecision.

"I'll even let you wear my jacket."

"Just what I've always wanted," she said, batting her eyelashes sarcastically, "a leather jacket to keep my skin from scraping off."

Laughter escaped. "Such a smart aleck."

"I have to be! You're intent on making me roadkill for the sake of getting to point B faster."

He leaned forward, staring into her eyes as he ran a finger down her cheek. "You can hold me tight so you don't become roadkill."

Delaney's mouth snapped shut and her cheeks brightened. "You're trouble, Luke Robinson."

"Nah," he scooted back some, "just a tad bit incorrigible."

"I'll say," she muttered.

The air filled with Tim McGraw's crooning voice. Time to lighten the mood again. He could always convince her to ride his bike later. He stood and held out a hand. "Dance with me?"

Delaney placed her soft hand in his and he helped her up, ushering her into his arms. She placed her hands on his shoulder as they began the shuffle perfected by middle schoolers across the country.

Slowly, they drifted closer as he hummed the melody. With a sigh, Delaney laid her head against his chest and slid both hands around his waist.

The tantalizing scent of her strawberry shampoo enveloped him as he nestled his chin in her hair. Song drifted into song, as they shuffled around. Time faded, but one thought remained.

There was nowhere else he wanted to be.

Lord, if you could somehow preserve this moment, I'd be forever grateful. He rubbed his cheek against the top of her head.

Somehow, fun had morphed into something much more meaningful. Life really couldn't get much better than this precise moment.

♡

Delaney's heart had lodged itself into her chest. She opened her mouth to break the silence and promptly shut it.

If she broke the silence, would the magic of tonight fade away? She kept her eyes trained outside as the scenery sped by, thinking of their date. It had been nothing short of amazing.

Luke had pulled out every trick in the romance hat: the lovely boat ride, the picnic, and even the music. She sighed, remembering the way he held her as they swayed back and forth.

All that was missing was moonlight.

She was actually surprised he hadn't managed to coordinate that somehow. Yet, none of it felt contrived. Luke was genuine. There was no question about that. No, that's not what rendered her mute at the moment.

It was the ache in her chest and the sighs that had escaped throughout the night. She had been utterly romanced, and it petrified her. Froze her vocal chords and rendered her speechless. Somehow, the desire to have fun had been overshadowed by the desire to feel loved. After all, wasn't that what romance was about? How could she let her heart melt at Luke's machinations when she knew he was going back in two weeks? *Two weeks!*

It would be here before she knew it. He would walk out of The Maple Pit and ride his motorcycle out on the horizon...or something to that effect. All she knew was he wasn't going to stay.

Uncle Sam beckoned.

Chills racked her frame at the thought. Even though she'd promised to keep things friendly, a little part of her already wanted to beg him to not go. To stay so that she could see where this would lead.

Wouldn't it be wonderful if he didn't have to stay in the military?

She wondered when his enlistment was up.

No, she couldn't ask. That was a clingy sign of desperation, and not something she wanted to exhibit. *Pull it together, Delaney. Erect those barriers!*

"Did you have fun?"

She turned toward Luke. "I did." She offered a smile, hoping he couldn't see her bruised heart. "You?"

He nodded. "I'd love to get together again. Maybe horseback riding?"

A memory pressed on the edge of present. She couldn't do something with him and her kids. It would make her feelings too real. "How about something else?" She snapped her fingers. "I could take you hiking."

His eyes crinkled. "That sounds good."

"Great, when's your next day off?"

"Whenever you'll go out with me."

She chuckled, hoping to cover the catch in her breath. Her heart felt like it was stuck in quick sand. If she didn't grab a life preserver, she would sink under the weight of his charm. "I think I have Tuesday off. I'll check and let you know."

"Sounds great."

He slowed, pulled her car up next to his Harley, and turned off the engine.

"Want to come in for some dessert?" She didn't want the date to end, despite being prepared to fly out the car and put a stop to it.

"Actually, I'm a little full. What about something to drink?" He nodded toward the porch. "We could occupy those chairs."

"All right. Sweet tea?"

"Perfect."

She headed inside and walked down the foyer toward the kitchen. Her mother looked up from a magazine. She was perched on a barstool. "How was your date?"

"Still going on." Delaney hooked a thumb over her shoulder, "He's outside. We're going to talk and drink some tea."

"I see." Her mother didn't even bother hiding her smirk. "I take it you're having a good evening."

"I am." She closed the fridge. "No need to wait up, Ma." *I'm a grown woman.*

"Pssh. Like everything is about you. I'm just reading my magazine." She held it up, an image of Oprah staring back.

"Hmm. Enjoy."

"You too, Delaney." Her mother snickered.

What is she insinuating?

Finding Love 115

Shaking her head, she headed back outside. Her mother's moods changed more than Virginian temperatures. She paused, noting Luke had maneuvered two chairs side by side. She handed him a glass and sat hers down on the bistro table to the left of her chair.

"Thank you."

"Sure." Delaney smoothed her dress under her legs and sat down. She stared at her hands, searching for a topic to discuss.

Tonight had been an easy mixture of talking and not. It was like her mind automatically knew which would be the better of the two. Only now, nerves were erasing her thoughts like the twist of an Etch A Sketch.

Was it because of the looming good night ritual? *Probably.*

She never knew if you should hug or kiss on the first date. Or worse, what if there was an option—like a handshake—that she never even imagined? It was absolute torture trying to figure it out. Did she want him to kiss her?

Yes.
No.
Maybe?

She exhaled. It was too soon for a goodnight kiss. Besides, he was leaving. *He's leaving. Don't forget.*

"I'm not going to kiss you good night."

"What?" She whipped her head around and met Luke's grin.

"Look at you. You're so tense I'm afraid you'll snap. No, ma'am. No kissing tonight."

"Like I wanted you to kiss me anyway, Luke Robinson."

He winked at her. "You did."

Blast! How did he do that? See straight into her soul?

"On a serious note, I like you too much to screw this up."

"Luke..." There was no way she could maintain her irritation. "We have to stay friends. You're leaving in two weeks."

He sighed and ran a hand across his jaw. What had been clean-shaven was now sporting a five o'clock shadow. "I know. Believe me, I know."

"What are we going to do?" she whispered.

"Take it one day at a time, Delaney."

She nodded as melancholy pressed down upon her.

"Walk me to my bike, please?"

"All right." She clasped his offered hand as they strolled to his bike.

It was amazing how his hand completely covered hers. He made her feel dainty, protected, and cherished. Parker had been an inch shorter, but she'd never minded. They were equals.

Being with Luke was different. He made her feel more feminine, and she never imagined herself as the ultra-feminine type.

He came to a stop and pulled her into his arms, resting his chin on her head. "Thanks for a wonderful evening," he murmured.

"It was wonderful." *But it has to end! You're leaving.*

"Don't overthink."

"I'll try not to." She sighed and pulled back. "Night, Luke."

"Sleep well, Delaney."

Chapter Thirteen

Unease skittered down Luke's spine. He glanced around the kitchen of The Pit, looking for something…anything to be amiss. Everything appeared to be normal.

Just like the other times he checked when the hairs on the back of his neck stood at attention. Something was off, but what?

Mrs. Williams pulled a cheesecake out of the fridge. Aimee, the new hire, stood to his right, dishing up the sides. And Alex…well it was his day off. He was probably listening to music blasting out of speakers or something.

Although there were hints here and there that made him wonder exactly how loud the music really was.

He sighed, wondering at the edgy feeling tingling along his spine. He didn't even enjoy the breakfast Ms. Bella cooked this morning.

The hairs on his arms stood at attention, like sensors checking for trouble. Praying didn't banish it. Reading his Bible didn't explain it. Calling his father and Gram assured him of their safety.

His eyes followed Delaney as she stopped at a table to hand them their check. She'd joked with him earlier and even made eye contact. Couldn't be her. *So what was it?* Mrs. Williams had been suspiciously silent. He thought for sure she'd give him the third degree or make comments about his date.

Not a peep had left her lips. That meant Delaney had kept quiet, or Mrs. Williams had decided to mind her own business. Both of those ideas seemed odd. He put the plate on the server's counter and began working on the next order.

In thirty minutes, the restaurant would close. Regulars and locals would slowly filter out as the staff worked to clean The Pit and ready it for the next day.

Perhaps he was simply tired. He hadn't slept well last night. His body had wavered between euphoria over a great date and sadness that his time in Maple Run would come to an end.

Despite praying daily, he was no closer to making a decision about his upcoming reenlistment. It seemed like a no-brainer. Enlist for two more years and earn a retirement paycheck from the Army.

Then he could move on to the next phase in life.

Simple enough.

Not.

His heart was tugging him toward Delaney, toward Maple Run and everything it stood for. The sense of family pulled at him, except Texas had his family, too.

How could he just up and leave his father and Gram behind? And for what? Some obscure feeling in the pit of his stomach every time a certain brown-eyed beauty looked at him?

It was nonsense. Ludicrous even.

The desire of your heart.

Finding Love

He blinked as the words echoed in his mind. Delaney was the desire of his heart. As the thought reverberated in his being, he sensed a rightness. He wanted a life with Delaney in it.

Only she was terrified of being with a soldier. How could he ask her to be with him, wait for him, when he was wearing the very uniform that made her stomach turn? It seemed needlessly cruel.

But he was a soldier.

Had been since he turned eighteen. It was all he knew. All he'd ever done.

Lord, I can't leave it unfinished. Two more years, Lord. That's all they're asking. How can I commit to that and commit to Delaney as well? She's what I want, Lord. Even though part of me is saying it's too early to know. I know. I just do. He sighed. *Please, give me wisdom. Please.*

"Dwight, what are you doing here?"

Luke turned at the sound of Mrs. Williams' voice. Her son stood in the doorway, his arm in a bright green cast.

"Bored. Thought I could help out."

Mrs. Williams snorted. "Not likely."

Luke looked down, trying not to eavesdrop.

"There's got to be something I can do, Mama."

"Yes, go home and spend some time with your wife and kids."

Dwight scowled, pacing like a caged lion. Poor man looked like he was going stir crazy. Luke had suffered many injuries in the past eighteen years, casualty of jumping out of aircrafts. Pity took hold. "We need more beef." He met Dwight's eyes. "Could you grab some?"

A look of relief flashed across Delaney's brother's face. "Got it." He left the kitchen in a hurry.

Mrs. Williams placed a hand on her hip. "Are you interfering, Luke?"

"No, ma'am. I would never do that. Since we have no meat in this fridge," he said pointing behind him, "and the only other meat is frozen, I figured you would want it to thaw tonight so it would be ready tomorrow. Was I wrong?"

He met her gaze, holding in his laughter at her exasperation.

"Very well, Luke. Why don't you go help him?"

Noting the time, he gave her a nod of agreement. No more orders would be coming in the kitchen.

When he entered the freezer, Dwight was in the back trying to juggle packs of meat in one hand. "Let me help you." He rushed to the man's side.

"Nah, I got it. Just close the lid for me." Dwight stepped back, using his casted hand to aid in balancing the meat.

Luke closed the lid and turned. Dwight was studying him with an intensity that unnerved him. The uneasy feeling came back full force.

"What's up with you and my sister?"

Uh oh. Not one of those conversations, Lord. "We're friends." He gulped as if he could actually swallow the nervousness down.

"Friends that go on boat rides and have picnics?"

Okay, apparently *Dwight* was the one Delaney talked to. "Yes. We're taking it one day at a time."

"Why?" Dwight asked bluntly.

"Why are we taking it one day at a time?"

"Yes."

Luke sighed. "You know her, so you must know my job is a road block."

"Is it for you?"

He shrugged. How was he supposed to answer that? Delaney would be the first person he told if he decided not to reenlist. Except she had no clue that was an option for him right now.

"I've got two years to retirement. I doubt she'll see that as a good thing."

Dwight nodded. "Yeah, she'll twist it in her brain and say two years' worth of opportunities for you to die."

He winced.

"Hey, man. I'm not trying to be cruel. You have to understand what Parker's death did to her."

"I get it. I've had friends and fellow soldiers die. I don't want to make it hard on her."

"Then don't you think it's best if you step away? You're gone in two weeks. How hard can it be to leave her alone for the rest of your stay?"

Considering they worked together? "Pretty difficult."

"Don't you want what's best for her? Because if you do, then I suggest you leave now." Dwight eyed him, irritation deepening the lines in his face.

Delaney inhaled sharply. Panic rose at the implications. Luke couldn't leave. Her heart pounded in her chest as Dwight's words sank in.

"No!"

Luke spun around and Dwight stared at her dumbfounded. She walked forward feeling like she was in a fog. "You can't leave. I thought we were friends." She stared at Luke willing him to understand.

Although she wasn't ready to put a name to her feelings, she wasn't ready for him to walk away either. Hearing Dwight ask him to leave caused an ache so intense it scared her with its force.

Didn't she want him to leave?

"We are friends." Luke said softly. "And I made a commitment to help out for the next two weeks."

Two weeks. It wasn't long enough. Her breath shuddered out. "So you won't leave?" *Me* went unsaid.

"Not now."

She pushed the thought of his impending departure away. "And you won't...avoid me?"

"Delaney," Dwight interrupted.

"Hush, Dwight." Her words held an edge barely recognizable. "I seem to remember getting a tongue lashing from you for interfering with your relationship with Nina."

Dwight sighed. "I'm out." He paused next to her, "Don't forget to pray about what you're doing, Dee."

She nodded, but her eyes never wavered from Luke's. The eyes that had captivated her from the first moment she met him. Eyes that seemed to see straight into her soul and heart. Eyes she could stare at for the rest of her life.

Whoa. She stepped back.

"Delaney," Luke ran a hand down the back of his head. "Your brother has a point."

"What?" *No.* He wasn't supposed to side with Dwight. "You just agreed we're friends."

"I did. We are." He gestured between the two of them. "What if our friendship goes down a road you're not prepared for?"

"Which is?" Her breathing came in short gasps. What was he trying to say? Her hands balled up as her teeth bit down on the inner portion of her lip.

"I like you, Delaney." Luke stepped forward. "A lot. But I'm leaving in two weeks to go back to work." His words were slow and steady giving her time to understand the implications.

He was in the Army.

They were just friends.

Neither thought brought comfort or clarity. Why was she so upset? How many times had she told herself the same thing? Yet, hearing it from his lips tore at her heart.

"What if I want more?" she whispered.

He took another step closer and took ahold of her hands. "Then you have to be certain it's what you want. I don't want you to have any regrets." His eyes searched hers as if searching for her decision.

"How will I know?"

"Only God can tell you."

"I don't want you to leave."

His eyes closed. "Delaney," he whispered. He lowered his head, touching his forehead to hers. His breath fanned gently against her face.

She wrapped her arms around him. "I don't know what to say, Luke."

"Then say nothing. I don't want you to agree to a relationship if you can't handle my job – if you can't handle the distance."

She wanted to cry in frustration. If she agreed to be in a relationship with him, what was the point if he was going to leave anyway? The inner turmoil spilled out, and she put voice to her thoughts.

"I get to pick my next assignment. Who's to say I can't come to Virginia?"

An ember of hope flared inside her. Could she be with another soldier? Go through the possible trauma of losing him? But wouldn't she lose him anyway if she said no?

Frustration coursed through her.

Luke pulled back slightly. "Go home." He brushed her hair away from her face. "Pray and when you know the answer, call me."

She nodded. "Okay."

"Can I walk you to your car?"

"Yes. Let me go get my stuff."

She rushed through the building and grabbed her purse out of the breakroom where the wall lockers were stored. By the time she had everything, Luke stood waiting for her by the back door. All the staff parked behind the building, leaving the front and sides for paying customers.

Her fingers shook as she looked for her keys. Tonight marked a turning point, but she wasn't sure to what exactly. Could she overcome her fear and date Luke? Or was it better to close her heart?

Lord, I need You. I don't know what to do.

The prayer rose and for a moment she wondered what His answer would be. What did God want for her in this life? And with whom?

A groan slipped out. The incessant questions needed to stop.

"You okay?"

"Thinking."

Luke squeezed her hand. "It'll be okay. Whatever you decide."

She stopped next to her car. "Will it? How do you know?"

"Because God's still God, Delaney. No matter what decisions we make, He's still good. And as long as He is good, we'll be good. Okay?"

"Okay." She offered a smile but her cheeks hurt from the force of it.

Luke leaned forward and brushed a kiss on her forehead. "Sleep well, Delaney."

He closed the car door for her and headed for his bike. She watched, noting his drooping shoulders. Despite the assurance he'd offered, it was obvious that this night was hitting him harder than he'd let on.

Part of her wanted to ask him if he would really move to Virginia for her. The other...the other was terrified he would say yes.

Because then you have to admit your feelings.

She laid her head against the steering wheel. *Lord, You know how I feel; do I really need to say it?* Ignoring the resounding "yes" that echoed in her head, she started the car and headed home.

Her questions would remain.

Her feelings weren't going anywhere.

It was time to go home and spend time with her boys.

Chapter Fourteen

Luke opened the front door to the B&B. His morning outing had been fruitful, and possibilities were popping up along the horizon. Bursting with news, he headed for Micah's guest room.

His friend was supposed to leave this morning but wanted to catch brunch at The Maple Pit first.

He knocked on the door. "Soup?"

"Yeah, come in."

Luke opened the door and leaned onto the doorframe. "You won't believe what I just found out."

Micah paused, looking up from tying his shoelaces. "What's that?"

"There's an opening for a skydiving instructor nearby."

"Skydiving?" Micah arched an eyebrow.

"Come on, I didn't jump out of perfectly good aircraft for nothing. The experience has to lead me somewhere."

"What about law enforcement? They love to hire vets."

He groaned. "You know I'm not law enforcement material." Not to mention, Delaney would probably hate that job even more.

"Why not? You follow rules."

"Nah, don't have the personality for it."

"But skydiving?"

"Hello, I jump out of planes for a living."

"Right." Micah said. "Big operation or small?"

"Small. One man owned. He's a vet as well. I talked to him about certification and whatnot. He thinks it'll take no time to get my military certifications transferred over to the civilian side. And he might have mentioned retiring in the near future."

"So what...he'll just sign the reigns over to you? Doesn't he have family?"

"Depends on how I work out. Nope, no family." He straightened up. This was a good deal; he could feel it in his bones. "What do you think?"

"It's not what I think, man. Is it what God wants?"

"I'm pretty sure. I've been praying all morning."

"How are you?" Micah stared at him.

Uh oh. "I'm good."

"Working at a restaurant hasn't been a problem? I mean with the alcohol?"

"It's a dry restaurant."

"Word?" Soup's eyebrows rose. "How is it possible they serve no alcohol?"

He chuckled. "That's God looking out."

"I'll say. Now I've really got to eat there."

"Let's go."

They headed outside.

"You going to introduce me to Delaney?"

"I don't know if she's working this morning. Besides, we're doing the whole one day at a time thing."

"But you want to move here."

"I do." He'd be crazy not to. The feelings Delaney evoked didn't come around every day. No, those were feelings that started a lifelong relationship.

"Have you told her about the year after Jones's death?"

Luke stopped, staring at his friend. "I told her life was hard."

"Understatement."

He folded his arms. "What are you saying?"

"You need to tell her about the drinking."

"Soup..."

Micah held his hands up. "Hear me out. If you want to do forever with this woman, then you need to open up about your past. She needs to know what she's dealing with."

"I haven't slipped up once, man."

"But you want to sometimes."

True. He squeezed his eyes shut, but it didn't block out Micah's words. Drinking had been on his mind every single day, all day, for a whole year.

When he made the choice to get sober, it was still a part of him, but not the controlling force. Now God took those reins, but it didn't erase the feelings of temptation every now and again.

"You're right."

"God's got you, Crusoe." Micah clapped him on the shoulder. "I'm sure everything will work out."

But what if it doesn't? Would Delaney end their friendship because he used to be a drunk and was a recovering alcoholic? As much as he wanted to downplay his past and make excuses, it didn't change what it was.

Just how many strikes could he accrue?

He got into Soup's truck.

"I see you worrying over there."

"It's not looking good, Soup. She already hates the fact that I'm a soldier."

"Ask yourself, if she had a demon in her past, would it change your feelings?"

No. The answer came hot and swift, but feelings weren't always a guaranteed reality. "No, but who knows what could happen when it comes down to it? You think you'll react one way, and a different response comes out of left field. If I were her, I'd be leery."

"When it comes down to it, all we can really do is trust in the Lord and let Him handle the rest. It's tough, but He won't steer us wrong, Crusoe."

"I know. It's the same advice I've given Delaney. It's just a little hard to remember at times."

"I feel ya."

"Change of subject," Luke said. "Did you get the job?"

"Sort of."

"What does that mean?"

"Dr. Kerrington wants to do a trial run. I have some leave at work I can use. At the end of the two-week period, he'll extend a full-time offer if we work well."

"When will you do the trial?"

"Not sure. I have to take a look at the schedule. Do you know how hard it is for a nurse to take some time off? They like to schedule vacation time *months* in advance."

"So, you're saying you have no idea if you'll get the job."

"Nope, I'm saying if it's meant to be, God will work everything out."

"It'd be kind of cool if you and I ended up in Maple Run. Crusoe and Soup back together again."

"Sounds like a B-rated movie."

Luke laughed. "Maybe, but we'll crack up laughing any way."

"Truth."

❤

Delaney held the door of The Pit open so that Preston and Philip could go through first. She scanned the restaurant, looking for Dwight and Nina.

"Mom, Uncle D is over there." Preston pointed to a corner booth.

Nina, Dwight, and the twins were situated in a huge corner booth. She followed the boys as they zipped through the tables, eager to join in the family breakfast. Sometimes, there were definite perks to being an owner of a restaurant.

"Hey there, sweetie." She bent down to tickle Gabe's chubby cheeks.

He lay nestled in Nina's arms. He grinned up at her, drool coursing down his chin and a little tooth peeking through his gum line.

"Oh, Nina, he has a tooth now."

Nina's lips curved into a bittersweet smile. "I know. Isn't it adorable?" She sniffed. "We noticed it yesterday. They grow so fast."

"They sure do." She kissed Gabe's chubby cheeks then slid into the booth. Her brother was bouncing her niece in his arms. "You going to hand over Abby?"

Dwight grinned as six-month-old Abby slapped his face with her chubby hands. "I suppose so, since you're throwing me eye daggers."

She rolled her eyes. "Whatever, little brother. Hand the baby over."

Abby clapped her hands and reached for her. "Hi, sweet Abby. You miss your Auntie?"

"Babababa," she babbled.

"Sounds like someone wants a bottle."

"More like she said, 'Da da.'" Dwight said with a grin.

"Sorry to burst your bubble, D, but she said it with a 'b'." She turned to Abby. "Isn't that right, sweet pea?"

"Mom, there's Mr. Luke."

Her head swiveled instinctively, searching for Luke. He was at the hostess stand, next to an African-American man who looked like he worked out.

"Who's he with?" Nina asked.

"No idea," she murmured. Her gaze roamed over Luke's tall frame.

He turned away from Nikki and spotted her. He waved and her cheeks warmed.

"Good grief, you've got it bad, girl," Nina muttered.

"Shh." She motioned for Luke to come over. "Please behave, Dwight."

"What?" His eyebrows rose in mock innocence. "I left you alone yesterday, didn't I?"

"After inserting your foot."

"Oh, I have to hear this story," Nina said, looking back and forth between them.

"Later," Dwight mumbled.

"Hey, Delaney," Luke said.

"Hi." She stared into his beautiful eyes.

"Hi, Mr. Luke!" Preston shouted.

"Hi...Preston, right?"

Preston nodded with a grin.

"How y'all doing?"

She grinned at the sound of his Texas drawl. "We're good. You?"

"Hungry." He motioned to the man standing beside him. "Delaney, this is my friend, Soup." At her blink, he grinned. "Call sign. Let me start over. Delaney, this is my friend, Micah Campbell. Micah, this is Delaney, Preston, Philip, Dwight, Nina, and their kids."

"Nice to meet everyone." Micah slid his hands into his pocket, an easy smile on his face.

"Likewise," she stated.

"Would you care to join us?" Dwight asked.

Delaney froze, trying not to glare at Dwight. Where exactly did he think they would fit?

"Um, thanks, but we can get our own table."

"Nonsense. How about you two sit here." Dwight continued. "Nina and I can take the kids and eat at another table."

Delaney aimed a kick at Dwight.

He glared at her.

Luke looked at her, a question in his eyes. "I don't want to interrupt a family breakfast."

"Oh, we see each other all the time. You're the one leaving soon." And with that, Dwight left the booth with Nina, a twin in each arm. He bent down toward her ear. "Makeup for inserting my foot." With a wink, he disappeared.

She was going to make sure her revenge on her little brother was perfectly timed.

"Sorry about that, Delaney."

"No worries." She gestured to the empty spaces. "Join us." She peeked at the boys. They didn't appear to be upset.

Luke slid in next to Philip and gave him an uneasy grin. He looked a little uncomfortable and for the first time, she realized she had no idea how he felt about kids. Were her boys another roadblock in their relationship?

She sighed. She needed to find out and fast.

After they placed their orders, Delaney leaned forward. "How do you two know each other?"

"Oh, I met Crusoe on deployment," Micah said.

"Really? What do you do?"

"I'm a flight nurse. Well, not entirely true. I used to be a flight nurse. Now I'm trying to find a job as a physician's assistant."

"What's a flight nurse?" Preston asked, his nose wrinkled up in confusion.

"Pres, you know better than to listen to grown-ups talk."

He rolled his eyes. "I don't have any food and nothing to color. *Of course,* I'm going to listen to you talk."

Luke chuckled. "I don't blame you. I want a coloring sheet, too."

Preston eyed him skeptically. "Why? You're old."

"I'm too old to color? Who told you that?"

"Grown-ups don't color." Preston stared in open-mouth astonishment.

"I do," she said. The boys gaped at her. She shrugged. "What? The adult coloring books are fun."

"See," Luke said. "Grown-ups like to color too."

"Crazy," Preston muttered. "I still want to know what a flight nurse is."

Micah grinned. "It's a nurse who gets to ride in a helicopter."

"Why do you do that?"

"Sometimes soldiers are hurt in a place we can't drive to. So the pilot flies to rescue them, and I patch them up and take care of them until we get to the hospital."

"Wow. That's kind of cool." Preston said in awe.

Delaney met Luke's gaze. Had he needed medical assistance? Or had he met Micah the regular way, bumping into each other on a post?

Luke seemed to read the question in her mind because he pointed to his arm.

He'd hurt his arm. She stared at the limb in question. Was it a gunshot wound? Her breath caught in her throat as her head swam under the possibilities.

"Hey, Micah, can you let me out a second?" Luke asked.

"Sure."

Luke slid out of the booth and offered her a hand. "Come with me for a second."

She stared at the boys and then at Micah.

"They'll be fine with me."

"Thank you." She placed her hand in Luke's, wondering if she wasn't already too far gone.

Chapter Fifteen

Luke headed for the breakroom. He could tell by the look in Delaney's eyes that she needed to know how he met Micah. He'd tried to silently convey that it had been an injury to his arm.

But that just added to the confusion on her face. If she was going to make a decision about his job, then she needed to know all the details.

Including the drinking?

He closed the breakroom door and leaned back against it. "I wasn't shot."

Breath whooshed out her body. "Thank God."

"Amen. My buddy tackled me to the ground to avoid a bullet and accidentally broke my arm."

"You were shot at?" Her voice reached new heights.

He winced. "I didn't get shot though."

"But you *were* shot at."

"Delaney…did your husband ever tell you he got shot at?"

She slowly nodded.

"So, you know it's a possibility."

"I forgot."

"I've only deployed six times since I've been in the military."

She folded her arms. "How long have you been in?"

"Eighteen years."

"You only have two years left?"

He paused. Did he nod or tell her he still needed to make a decision? "Two more years and I can retire."

"Wait, how old are you?"

How had they not had this discussion already? *Hormones.* "I'll be thirty-seven in December."

She bit her lip.

"Is that a bad thing?"

"I hit thirty-seven last month."

"I like older women." He winked at her and laughed out right when her cheeks flamed bright.

"I'm not that much older." The whine in her voice was slightly adorable. "What do you plan on doing once you retire?"

"That's what I've been praying about." Should he mention the skydiving? *Nah, not yet.* Luke cleared his throat. "I'm not sure yet. Something that will use my business degree."

"Really?"

"Yes, ma'am. I do have business skills and managerial ones to boot."

"And you wouldn't get shot at."

"True." Ah, he knew it. She'd freak if he'd chosen law enforcement as a career path. When he joined the Army at eighteen, thirty-eight seemed a long way off.

Deep down, he'd expected to die in the military or go back to Texas until he could figure it out. "Micah suggested law enforcement or the Guard. Those guys only work on the weekends and have a normal job during the week."

And he could still retire.
"Doesn't the Guard deploy?"
"Sometimes."
She shook her head. "No, don't do that." She slapped a hand across her mouth. "I'm sorry, it's not like I have a say so."
But you do! He clenched his teeth from shouting his thoughts. If she only knew how much power she had over his choices. "It's okay. I value your opinion."
"You shouldn't."
"Delaney…"
"No, let me finish." She held up a hand and took a breath. "I like you, Luke, but this all feels kind of fast. You can't put your life on hold because of what I may or may not feel. Not only that, but who's to say this could ever work between us?"
"Why couldn't it?"
Her mouth dropped.
"If you take my job away, what other objections do you have?" *Tell her about the alcohol.*
She blinked at him and his heart picked up a cadence akin to the one he felt when he found a roadside IED. "Is it…" He paused not sure how to voice it.
"What?" she asked softly.
"Is it because I'm white?"
She laughed.
"Why is that funny?"
"I'm sorry. Of all the things I thought you would say that's not one of them."
"Okay, but some people have a problem dating outside of their race."
"If I was one of them, I would have never gone out with you in the first place." She lifted a shoulder. "Besides, color is the last thing I'm thinking about when I look at you."

Hearing the sincerity in her voice lifted a weight off his shoulder. He didn't realize how worried he was. Growing up in west Texas gave one a bird's eye view on race relations.

There were those stuck in the past, those who acted like it was no longer a problem, and everyone else.

Being in the military had given him the opportunity to appreciate a diverse group of people, but he knew to some African Americans, he would always be white.

"Then what other objections do you have?"

"Do you like kids?" she blurted out.

"Sort of."

Her eyebrows rose. "What does that mean?"

"I think kids are awesome. Smart. Funny even. I just have no idea how to act around them. They seem so...fragile."

"My kids won't break. If anything, they're likely to break something."

"Do you want more kids?"

Her eyes widened and a panic look filled them.

"I thought they weren't scary?"

"Having a kid when I'm knocking on forty is terrifying."

"So no more kids." He laced his fingers through hers. "Does that mean more time for us?"

"Wait...how did this conversation turn? You're acting like we're..."

"Discussing marriage?"

She nodded, her chocolate eyes focused on him.

"Well, aren't you worried you'll invest time in our relationship and it won't work out?"

"Yes, but..."

"Then we have to find out what the deal breakers are. We already know my job is one. Talking about kids and the rest is a step in the right direction."

She bit her lip. "I hear you, but it's too fast, Luke. We haven't even kissed yet."

His stomach jumped at her words. "I could change that."

Her gaze dropped to his mouth.

"If you don't stop staring at me like that, I'm going to change it with a quickness."

Delaney dropped his hands and stepped back. "No. I…if I agree to give this a shot we can seal it with a kiss."

He nodded, disappointment flooding through him. "Fair enough."

"We should go back and sit."

"All right."

As he followed her back to the dining area, unease coiled in his body. He hadn't mentioned the drinking. It was obvious she was already overwhelmed, but he needed to tell her before his heart was too entangled.

Too late.

"Mama, someone's at the door."

Delaney blinked in confusion. She hadn't heard the doorbell ring. "Thanks, Pres. I'll get it."

He grinned, showcasing a mixture of baby and adult teeth. She ruffled his head as she padded down the hall. As she came down the stairs, she slowed.

A view of a silhouette was visible through the glass pane to the right of the door.

Understanding flooded through her sleep-addled brain. She was dreaming. *Again.* It was Parker's dream, but something was different. Off. Unable to wake up, her dream continued.

"Who on earth?" she murmured. Going up on her tiptoes, she looked through the peephole.

Micah stood outside in his Army dress uniform.

Her mouth began to water and beads of perspiration popped across her forehead. Her hand shook as she reached for the door. She fumbled for the doorknob as tears blurred her vision.

Not again, not again, not again.

Slowly, the door opened. The abject misery on Micah's face twisted her insides.

"Where's Luke?" she croaked out.

"Can I come in, Delaney?"

She shook her head vigorously, wrapping her arms around her waist. "Where is he?"

"Delaney," Micah stated. "Let's go sit down in the living room."

He slowly entered the foyer, guiding her by the elbow toward her living room. Instead of being the home she had lived in with Parker, it had morphed into her childhood home.

The throw blanket was draped on the recliner where her mother liked to curl up and watch Westerns.

Wake up!

Micah squatted in front of her. "Delaney," he began. He cleared his throat then met her gaze head on. "I'm sorry to inform you, but Luke was killed."

Delaney shot up in bed, tears streaming down her face. She covered her mouth choking back sobs. Her heart felt like it was ripping in half. The ache in her chest was so intense she almost thought she was having a heart attack.

"Delaney?" Her mother's voice came through the door. "Delaney?" A knock on the door.

Tears coursed down her face and her body shook. Calling out to her mother was impossible. The door opened and her mother rushed in, concern deepening the crow's feet.

"What in the world?" Her mother wrapped her arms around her and rubbed her back.

Delaney buried her face in her mother's arms, thankful for the comfort. No matter how old she was, she could count on her mother. The sobs slowed as her heart began the descent into normal heart range.

"It's been a long time since dreaming about Parker has affected you so."

She slid away, using the edge of her shirt to wipe her face. "It wasn't Parker."

"What? Then what were you dreaming about?"

"It was the same dream except it was Luke who died."

She met her mother's gaze and paused. There was a peculiar look on her face, one Delaney couldn't quite describe. "What, Ma?" Her voice was scratchy from crying and sounded raw.

Considering how painful her throat was, she wasn't too surprised.

"It was the same dream except they told you Luke died?" Her mother's voice was quiet.

"Yes. Well, it was Micah who showed up instead of the Major."

"Interesting."

She sniffed back remnants of her tears. "Why?"

"You were sobbing your little heart out there. Don't you find that interesting?"

"I don't know about interesting," she said, wiping remnants of tears, "but it certainly answers my question."

"Which is what?"

"Can I handle his job? I'd take this dream as a no."

"Or perhaps…" Her mother paused. "Perhaps you can. Maybe the point of the dream is to show you how you feel already. Wouldn't you wonder what could be?"

She stared at her hands. Hadn't that been one of the questions she asked herself?

"Ma, I don't want another knock on my door telling me someone I love is dead. It's better to leave things as friends before it gets worse and I can't say good-bye."

"Can you say good-bye now?" Her mother stood up. "Don't be so quick to assume he'll end up in a casket, Delaney. Have faith."

With that her mother walked out and shut the door.

She wasn't sure how long she sat there staring at the closed door. Was she lacking faith? Did this relationship even have anything to do with God?

"I'm so confused, Lord," she whispered. "I knew that You wanted me to be with Parker. Saying 'yes' was the easiest thing I've ever done. But this isn't. I can't help but feel that it's a sign we shouldn't even try."

What did she know about Luke? She shook her head. Okay, so that was the point of dating. Why couldn't she just decide to date him and let the chips fall?

Because if it ended up with her receiving another set of widow's benefits, she would be crushed. Sink into another bottomless pit of depression and heartache. And she had her boys to think about.

Do you really? Not once have you thought about them other than to keep them away from Luke.

She grimaced. It's not that she was ashamed of them. Just didn't want them to get attached and then have another man ripped from their arms. Okay, so children often proved to be more resilient than adults. That didn't mean they wouldn't be affected. She grabbed her cell phone and pulled up her Bible app. Maybe she could find something to confirm her feelings.

She paused as the verse of the day popped up. *Matthew 9:29, "Then touched he their eyes, saying, 'According to your faith be it unto you.'"*

"Are you trying to tell me something?"

Goosebumps raised the hair on her arms. She couldn't stop staring at the verse. "According to my faith…" she murmured. "Are you trying to tell me the quality of my life is based on my faith?"

A tear slid down her face at the thought. Since Parker died, her quality of life was severely lacking. Using the words of her twins, "it sucked." Was it her lack of faith that caused her to dread each day?

To feel like she was stuck in tar and struggling to move forward?

Yet, with one look into dreamy blue eyes, she'd felt a glimmer. A spark of what could be.

"I'm scared, God. I don't want to give my heart and lose it again."

"The LORD is thy keeper."

She froze as the words resonated in her soul. God was the keeper of her heart, keeper of her entire being. She needed to let God hold her heart. Let Him dictate her actions and not rely heavily upon her feelings.

"Please help me, Lord. Show me what to do."

Chapter Sixteen

Sleep had eluded him for the better part of the night. Now that morning had arrived, he wanted nothing more than to crawl under the covers and sleep the day away.

Except his brain still wouldn't shut up. It insisted on going through different scenarios.

Enlist or not?

Guard or no Guard?

And when to tell Delaney about his sobriety?

If he reenlisted, Delaney would still have to come to terms with his job. Same if he crossed into the Guard.

Of course, if he chose to just separate, her peace of mind would be assured. But no retirement check.

"Money's not everything, Son."

He winced as his father's words echoed in his brain.

Okay, so money wasn't everything. If he ended up owning the skydiving business, it may be enough to take care of him until he decided to retire from working.

God, could you please just tell me what to do already?

And what if He had, and Luke missed it because he was constantly pleading to God instead of listening?

Ouch. He ran a hand across his chin. Okay, he needed to be quiet. His phone chimed, signaling an incoming text from Delaney. He opened it.

You up?

Yes. You okay? His thumbs flew across the screen.

Yes. Can I come see you?

His eyebrows rose. Did she have good news or bad news?

Sure. Ms. Bella's making breakfast if you're hungry.

No, been up since 6. Already ate.

He laughed. She could have texted him then too. Nothing like insomnia to bond a couple. Then again, her boys were early risers.

Be there in a bit.

K.

He stood up, tossing his phone on the bed. It would take him no time to be presentable. The military had taught him how to get ready in a hurry. By the time she pulled up to the B&B, he'd be ready.

The size of the town guaranteed she'd arrive soon.

As he finished tying his boots, a knock sounded.

"Visitor, Mr. Robinson."

"Thanks, Ms. Bella," he called out.

"Please let it be good news, Lord." He ran a hand over his face and took a deep breath before exiting his room.

Delaney was waiting for him in the living room, sitting on the couch. She had on a gauze tank top and shorts, looking just as beautiful as ever. *Don't let her break my heart, Lord.* "Hey."

"Hi," she smiled.

"Want to go sit on the porch?" *That way if you kick me in the gut, Ms. Bella won't be a witness.*

"Sure."

He headed for the front. His stomach felt like it was doing the rhumba. Thank goodness he hadn't eaten yet.

If so, it would probably be working its way back up. He slid his hands down his jeans before opening the door.

Nerves were going to put his deodorant to the test. Just yesterday she seemed so hesitant and heart broken. Now there was a peace around her.

A peace that signified a decision had been made. *But which one?*

His stomach clenched. "Have a seat." He gestured to one of the rocking chairs.

"How about the porch swing?" She pointed to the white wooden seat covered in pillows.

A pulse in his neck jumped. "You want to sit on the porch swing? Together?"

Delaney laughed and grabbed his hand. "Come sit with me."

He followed, almost stumbling over his feet. *Why was she so happy?* What had happened between last night and this morning? Obviously, she'd gotten way more sleep than he did.

She patted the space beside her and he sank down into it. He stared at his arms wondering if he should put them around her or the swing. He slipped one on the back of the swing, trying to relax.

Delaney smiled up at him and scooted into the crook of his arm.

That's a good thing, right, Lord?

"I need to tell you about my night."

"Okay," he said cautiously. His heart was thumping like crazy in his chest. Being this near to her was overloading his senses.

"I have this reoccurring dream about Parker. Well, it's more like a memory, except I dreamt about it."

He squeezed her shoulder in comfort.

"Anyway, I had it again last night, but it was different."

"Different how?"

"First, let me tell you how it usually goes."

He nodded and listened as she relayed the dream. His jaw clenched. Bad memories were hard enough to overcome, but to relive it over and over in a dream? He shook his head. She was tougher than she realized.

"That's usually how it goes."

"How was last night's dream different?"

"Micah was at my door."

"What?" He straightened up and met her gaze. She had a dream he died? He wanted to groan in frustration. No way this would bode well.

"My thoughts exactly. Only I couldn't wake up and the dream played on until Micah told me you died."

"Oh, Delaney." The words tore from his heart. He ran a hand down his face. This was *not* good. Should he just let her go now before he caused more heartache? He nestled his head against her hair. "I'm so sorry."

He ached to say more, but what?

"No." She looked up at him. "It was a good thing."

"How?"

"Because it finally made me realize I've been lacking faith." She went on and told him about the Bible verse and how it affected her. "Luke, I don't want to merely live and go through each day in a mutinous state of being. I want more."

What was she saying? "More what?" He swallowed, trying to hold the hope back.

"More out of life. I want to see where this thing between us goes."

"Really?" Relief flooded through him. He felt like a wet noodle. "You really do?"

"I really do." She beamed at him.

"My job's not a problem?"

"No."

"Are you sure?" Why couldn't he leave it alone? "If I decided to not retire at twenty and continued serving, you'd still be okay?"

She framed his face with her hands and brushed her lips against his. It was over so fast, he blinked.

"Yes," she breathed, her breath fanning his lips. "I'm okay with it."

"Thank God." His lips found hers again, and this time he took his time.

Life was great. Now that Delaney made the commitment to date Luke, she could breathe easier. Last night's rest had been dream free. She pulled her hair up into a ponytail as her mind continued to think about the handsome Texan.

How would she handle it when Luke had to leave?

No, worry about that later. She could do the whole crossing-that-bridge thing when it happened. She sighed as she turned sideways in front of the floor-length mirror making sure she looked okay.

You're just going hiking, Dee.

Still, it couldn't hurt to look her best. She couldn't wait to show Luke one of her favorite hiking places. He asked her to bring the kids along, but she declined. She knew eventually they would have to do family activities, but she wasn't ready.

You're still holding back.
"I'm not," she mumbled.
Luke was leaving in less than two weeks. She wanted to maximize their time together, which couldn't be done if Preston and Philip were around. Besides, what if something...no, she wouldn't go down that path. *See, holding back.*
"I'm not."
"You're not what?"
She yelped at the sound of her mother's voice. "Ma, you scared me."
"Probably because you're talking to yourself." Her mother folded her arms and leaned against the doorframe. "Why are you dressed like that for a date?" Her mother pointed to the shorts and T-shirt she was wearing.
"We're going hiking at Great Falls."
"Oh my goodness, I can't believe you found a guy who will hike with you."
She grinned. She couldn't help it. Luke was such an amazing man and now that she made the decision to see their relationship through, she could count the ways he interested her. *Like taking me hiking.*
"I think the first date was the best, but I want to show him the falls."
"Hmmm."
Great. Her mother didn't use that tone very often, but when she did, nothing good followed. She tied her hiking boots, doing her best to ignore her.
"Delaney."
She held back a sigh. "Yes, Ma?"
"You're not diving in head-first are you?"
"What do you mean?" She met her mother's concerned gaze.

"I want you to date, but it seems like you want to do more than that."

"Come again? I'm a Christian, Mother."

"Not that." Her mother waved a hand. "I meant it seemed like you were thinking wedding bells. You had the same look on your face you used to have when you were with Parker. The love look."

"Ma, no one has said the "L" word." *Even though we discussed kids already.* No way would she let that thought fly and have her mother dig deeper.

"I just wanted to remind you he's leaving soon. No need to get attached."

"Didn't you point out last night that maybe I was already attached?"

"I just meant you obviously *like* the boy. But now…now I see something different."

"I'm a grown woman, Ma. I have kids of my own, you know?"

"Look, Miss Thang. That man is headed back to the military. He doesn't live here and probably won't."

"He actually was talking about trying to move out here."

Her mother raised her eyebrows as her mouth dropped open. Dee went up to her and put her arms around her mother. "I won't move too fast. Don't worry."

"Too late," her mother mumbled.

"Ma, I'm a big girl. I'm okay."

"Says the 'big girl' who was crying her little eyes out the other night."

She sighed. "And didn't you tell me to acknowledge my feelings? What's with the big switch-a-roo?"

"I just worry."

"Don't. Please."

Finding Love

The doorbell chimed.

"That's him. Are we good?" She paused and looked her mother in the eyes.

"Have fun," her mother said begrudgingly.

"Okay."

She grabbed her rucksack and headed for the front door. The boys had spent last night at Dwight's house. Kandi was going to take them to a local trampoline place and let them bounce themselves into exhaustion.

She snickered, it wouldn't work, but it was a nice thought.

Luke stood in front of the door, his leather jacket unzipped in the blazing sunlight. He grinned, deep grooves appearing in his clean-shaven cheeks. "Hey."

"Good morning." She closed the door behind her. "We're riding the motorcycle, aren't we?"

He held out a helmet. "Of course we are."

She shook her head in bemusement. "I'm not so sure…"

"It'll be fine. I'll keep you safe."

Goosebumps appeared at the look in his eyes. She was sure he meant it, but who was going to keep her heart safe?

"Come on." He held out a hand, and she clasped it.

Her feet grew heavy as she walked closer to his bike. She'd never been on a motorcycle before. *Never.* What if she fell? What if she scraped her skin up? *Oh no.*

"I don't have a leather jacket." Relief flooded through her. They would have to take her car now.

Luke grinned and opened a compartment. He pulled out a caramel colored leather jacket. "Bought you one."

"You did?" Why was she charmed? Shouldn't she be irritated that she had no choice but to ride it now? "What about my legs?"

"I won't go that fast. I promise, I'll keep you safe."

Her heart dipped.

He held out the jacket, and she slipped it on. It was a perfect fit. "It's so smooth."

"First leather jacket?"

"Yes." Too bad there wasn't a mirror.

"You look good." His grin was wide, so she'd take it she looked better than good.

"All right. Tell me what I need to do."

For the next few minutes he went over instructions, like how to lean. He made sure she was comfortable before he started the bike. She leaned forward, wrapping her arms around his waist.

A sigh escaped her lips. She could get used to this.

"Hang on."

She nodded against his back, and he pulled away. Her hands clinched his waist, surprised by the movement. *Please, don't let us die, Lord. That would really suck.*

Slowly but surely, the tension fled and exhilaration took its place. Before long, Luke parked in the Great Falls parking lot. He put his feet down and took off his helmet.

"Well?" His ice blue eyes twinkled.

"Fantastic."

"I knew you'd like it."

She grinned. "Wait until you see the falls. It's the perfect follow up."

"No, this is." He pulled her close and kissed her softly on the lips.

Chapter Seventeen

Sounds of "Crazy Girl" filled the air as Luke's cell rang. A grin slipped over his face. Delaney was the only one with that ringtone. "Hey."

"I have a huge favor to ask you."

His gut clenched at the frantic sound of her voice. "What's wrong? Is someone hurt?"

"No. Shaunice is sick, and Ma needs me to serve for dinner. I'm so sorry. I know we were going out and everything…"

"No worries. What do you need me to do?" He didn't want to go in and cook, but if he got to be with Delaney, so be it.

"Could you possibly watch the boys for me?" A pause then Delaney's voice filled the air again. "Normally, I'd ask Kandi, but Dwight and Nina took her to college. She's doing some summer program and has to be there earlier than the rest."

"Well, first week of July is certainly earlier."

"I know."

Could he watch her boys? He hadn't had an opportunity to be around them. Delaney seemed to be keeping them at a distance, which he understood, despite the unease that ran through him at the thought. Guess now she had no choice. "Of course I'll watch them."

"Thank you so much. Can you come over like five minutes ago?"

"Sure." He chuckled. "Be there in a few."

In no time, he stood on her front porch, knocking on her front door, nerves drumming through him. What did nine-year-old boys like to do? *What did you like to do?*

Delaney opened the door looking flustered and harried. "Thank you so much, Luke."

"No problem."

"Come on in." She motioned him inside. "I'll introduce you to the boys again. They have different color shirts on so it should be easy to keep them straight. Preston's wearing red and Philip's wearing blue." She took a breath then yelled. "Preston! Philip!"

He raised his eyebrows. "Not only can you whistle, but you yell like a drill sergeant."

"Not exactly lady-like attributes," she shrugged.

Footsteps thundered as the boys appeared from the stairs below. He leaned close and whispered. "It's not like you belched. Besides, you have two boys. Those skills come in handy."

She smiled at him then looked at her boys.

"You guys remember Mr. Luke, right?"

"Hi!" They said in unison.

"Howdy."

"Mr. Luke's going to watch you while I'm at work. Be good and listen to him, okay?"

"Yes, ma'am."

"Okay. Give me a hug." She gave them each a hug, ruffling their hair afterward. They ran back downstairs.

She turned to him. "Bedtime is at nine. I just put a casserole in the oven, and it should be done in another…" she checked her watch. "Fifteen minutes. They have no allergies, no meds. Just make sure they don't kill each other or destroy anything in the house."

He laughed. "All right."

She leaned forward, placing her hands on his face. "Don't be worried. You'll be fine."

"Does the fear show?"

"Badly. Kids smell it better than animals."

Great. He laid a quick kiss on her lips. "Go before your mom panics."

"I'm going, I'm going."

Without a backwards glance, she was gone, and he was left standing in the foyer. He looked down the stairs. Did the light darken or was it his imagination?

Come on, Robinson. Just your fear. Shake it off and go babysit.

He could do this. Sending a quick prayer upward, he jogged down the stairs and entered mayhem.

Toys littered the *entire* basement floor.

Legos. Action figures. Dinosaurs.

Everything had made it onto the floor. Philip and Preston had donned Ninja Turtle masks and were using light sabers to fight as they each stood in an empty toy chest, yelling "Arrrrh" to one another.

Their characters were seriously mixed up. Probably couldn't find the right equipment in all the mess.

No way Delaney had seen this. She looked like the type of mom to blow a gasket and demand no supper until everything was back in its proper place.

And they had fifteen minutes until the casserole would be ready.

He clapped his hands. "Guys, let's clean up."

Nothing.

Their whoops and hollers drowned out his paltry attempt at an authoritative voice. It was time to use his non-commissioned officer voice. "Time to clean up!"

The sound of his voice echoed in the basement, freezing the boys mid-fight. Slowly, they turned and met his gaze.

"You sound like thunder!" Preston exclaimed.

"Had to use my sergeant's voice. Y'all are making too much noise to hear a person talk."

Philip looked sheepish. "That's what mom usually says."

"Well, your mom's right. Dinner's going to be ready in about fifteen minutes. Let's get this placed cleaned up before we eat."

"Then what will we play with after dinner if we put all the toys away?" whined Preston.

"Just listen," muttered Philip.

Luke tried to suppress his laughter at Preston's look of horror and annoyance. "Preston, we'll figure that out after dinner. But now we need to clean up."

He crossed his arms. "I don't want to."

Judging by the look on Philip's face, this wasn't Preston's normal behavior. Before he could admonish the kid, Preston stomped his foot and promptly let out a howl. "Ow! I stepped on a Lego." Tears darkened his brown eyes.

"Bet you want to help me clean up now." Philip remarked.

"You going to live, kid?" Luke asked.

Preston nodded.

"Good. Help Philip clean up. When y'all are done, wash your hands and come eat."

"Yes, sir," they mumbled.

He turned to head back upstairs and let his grin go free.
Nothing like stepping on a Lego to convince a kid to keep the floor toy free. He watched the time to ensure the casserole would be ready and that the kids weren't lollygagging.
Fortunately, they came upstairs right when the timer went off.
After saying grace, Luke took a bite of the maple-sausage and egg casserole. It'd been a while since he had breakfast for dinner.
The boys took a piece after drizzling their portion with syrup. He shuddered. That was entirely too much sweetness for him, but he wasn't a little kid anymore. His taste buds had matured.
At least, he thought so.
"How's your summer going?" He looked at them, hoping to entice them into a conversation.
"Great!" Preston said with a grin. He had two missing canines. "I'm so glad school's over. Too bad summer can't last forever. It's awesome, and tomorrow we're supposed to go on a Scout trip." He stuffed a spoonful of food into his mouth.
"Nice. Are you going camping?"
Preston nodded as he chewed, cheeks puffing out like chipmunks.
"Do you love our mom?" Philip stared at him, his food untouched.
Luke lowered his fork back to his plate. "That's why we're dating. To find out if we could love one another."
"Do you think if you loved her you'd love us? I mean…" he stammered, his face turning pink like his mother's. "Do you think you'd love us like a dad would love his kids?"

His heart turned over. All of a sudden, his fears seemed unfounded. How could he not love these kids? "Without a doubt."

"What does that mean?" Preston asked, his brow scrunching up with confusion.

"It means yes. Right?" Philip asked.

"Right."

Philip picked up his spoon and began eating. Luke watched them as silence descended. Delaney had two kids to think about. It was time to tell her about his drinking.

Delaney closed the front door quietly behind her. The boys should be asleep, but still, she didn't want to wake them if they were in dreamland. She walked through the foyer, wondering where Luke was.

A glance toward the kitchen told her it was unoccupied. A glance toward the left pulled her up short.

Luke was fast asleep on the floor. A book lay on his stomach as if he had fallen asleep while reading it. Philip and Preston were each at his side, dead to the world and wrapped up in their blankets from their room.

He was the sweetest man on earth. And she loved him.

She blinked rapidly and took a step back. She *couldn't* love him. Not now, it was way too soon. He would leave this weekend. Back to the military. Back to Georgia where he was stationed.

Lord, please don't let this relationship end like my last one. Unease slithered up her spine and cloyed its way around her throat. It tightened with unshed tears as fear pressed upon her.

Luke shifted, his eyes slowly blinking open. "Delaney?"

His voice washed over her, bringing peace in its wake. "Hey, sleepyhead." She cleared her throat. "Reading tires you out, huh?" She kept her voice low. Hopefully, the boys would stay asleep.

A wry grin slipped over his shadowed cheeks, deepening the grooves. "Your boys wore me out. We had the longest Uno match known to mankind."

She chuckled. There had been many times she wanted to cry uncle just to end a game, but her boys loved playing it, and seeing them happy was worth it. She held out her hand.

"Want to share a dessert with me?"

"Love to."

He stood up and pulled her close in one fluid motion. He slid his hands in her hair and cradled the back of her head as his lips met hers. Time slipped away and love slid firmly into her heart.

Into her soul.

She sighed, as contentment and peace weaved through her being.

Luke pulled back and smiled at her. "The best dessert ever."

Her face heated up and a chuckle escaped. "I have actual dessert." She grabbed his hand and headed for the kitchen. "Cheesecake or bread pudding?"

"Oh man," he said with a moan. "What kind?"

"Maple-bacon cheesecake, because really that's the only kind that counts." She winked. "But the bread pudding is pretty stellar. My mom makes it with a maple-pecan sauce."

"Hmm, I'll try the bread pudding."

She sat the plates down after preparing each of them a slice of the pudding.

"I thought for sure you'd get cheesecake."

She shrugged. "Sometimes you need something different."

"I agree." His blue eyes stared straight into her soul.

A sappy grin found its way onto her face. This man was turning her into a mushy pile of girl hormones. She took a bite of her dessert to keep her expressions of love to herself.

No sense in scaring him off.

"Delaney."

"Hmm?"

"I need to tell you something."

She quickly swallowed her bite of food. "What's wrong?"

"It's about my life after Jones died."

"What?" He was scaring her big time.

"Remember I told you their deaths hit me kind of hard?"

She nodded, too afraid to speak past the pounding in her chest.

"I coped with alcohol." He stared at her, remorse darkening his blue eyes. "I drowned my guilt with any liquor I could get my hands on until the Army gave me an ultimatum."

"What are you saying?" She licked her lips, trying to make sense of his revelation.

"I'm a recovering alcoholic."

"How long have you been sober?"

"Two years, three months, and five days."

Whoa. She sat back, stunned. "Why are you telling me this?"

"Because you need to know it could be a problem in the future."

"Have you relapsed?"

"No, but the temptation still comes on every now and again."

"I..." *Don't know what to think!*

"You don't have to say anything right now, and I'll understand if you want me to leave."

"No," she breathed out. Leaving wasn't the answer. "I don't want you to leave."

A look of relief washed over his face. "Great."

"Hold up." She paused, gathering her thoughts. "You can't hold back, Luke. In a relationship, you tell all, bare all. I have to know you aren't going to hold out on me."

"Understood."

She took a bite of her food, thankful to get back to it. Luke tapped his fingers against the countertop, watching her. "Then I suppose there's one more thing I should tell you. I'm going to get out of the Army."

Her food sputtered everywhere. "Come again?"

"When my leave is up, I have to either reenlist for the next two years or turn in my separation papers. If I chose to separate I'll get out at the end of August."

Her heart stuttered in her chest. *Why hadn't he said anything?*

The question must have been evident on her face. "I didn't say anything because I didn't want to influence your decision about giving us a chance. Plus, I wasn't entirely sure I would get out."

"Okay, that's logic I can't argue with."

"There's a guy who owns a skydiving business that's willing to train me to take over so he can retire. If I want."

"Seriously?" *Skydiving?*

"Yes." He ran a hand across his cheek. "How does that sound to you?"

"Which part?"

"All of it."

"I need to think about the drinking."

He nodded.

"Getting out of the military sounds fantastic."

Luke grinned.

"But skydiving?"

"I won't get shot at, and I get to use the skills I acquired in the military."

"True." *He won't be a soldier anymore.*

She got up, rounded the island and threw her arms around his neck. "I don't care. Just the fact that you won't be in the Army any more is enough to excite me."

He chuckled and kissed her quickly on the lips. "Glad I could make you happy."

"You make me more than happy. I …" she smiled, biting off the words her heart yearned to scream. *Slow down, Delaney. You've only known him a month.* "I'm glad you're getting out."

"Me too. I can't imagine going back and worrying about whether I got stationed here. I don't want to chance it. I want to be here with you."

Did that mean he felt the same way? How she wished she could ask, but inexplicable fear stopped her. For now, it was enough that he wanted to move to Virginia and continue their relationship.

Chapter Eighteen

When he stopped at The Maple Pit for the very first time, Luke had no clue how the trip would change his life. Now, he couldn't imagine life without seeing the familiar faces.

Without hearing Delaney's voice every day.

He groaned, as he put his razors in the toiletry bag.

Unfortunately, time waited for no one, and now reality waited.

He had a few days to make it back to Texas and spend some time with his family before hopping on a plane to go back to his Army post in Georgia.

Of course, he could extend his stay at the B&B. He glanced around the room that had been his home for the last few weeks. The French doors beckoned, begging him to step outside and sit awhile.

Only he promised his Gram he would see her, and he was a man of his word. But man, oh man, did he want to stay.

How could he say good-bye to Delaney even if it was temporary?

Finally, he understood why some of the soldiers moped around the first couple of weeks of deployment.

They were missing their better half. Luke stared at his cell background.

Delaney's beaming face stared back at him. When he got on his Harley and drove away, he'd be leaving part of his heart. Leaving her.

Although he hadn't made any professions of love, it was there. Not that he would entirely admit it. Life still seemed precarious.

When he confessed his love, he wanted to be able to offer Delaney a comfortable life. As soon as he got back to the fort, he'd hand in his separation paperwork.

Jacobs wanted him to start the necessary paperwork to transfer his military certifications to the civilian world. It would be great sharing the joy of skydiving.

Of course, he had to view it from freefalling for the sheer joy of it versus to start an op. The smoother the transition, the quicker he could find himself back in Maple Run.

Which was why he arrived at Delaney's house bright and early. If he waited until this afternoon to leave, it would only prolong the pain. No, he was going to get it over with, sort of like ripping off a bandage.

Please don't let her cry, Lord.

She had texted him a minute ago that she would be downstairs soon. He didn't want to ring the doorbell.

Yesterday, he said his goodbyes to her mother, brother, and the boys. Preston had looked sad, but when Luke promised to be back in a couple of months, Pres perked right up. Philip just gave him a hug.

The door opened and Delaney paused on the threshold looking beautiful, but miserable. She flew into his arms, squeezing him tight. He stroked her hair and relished the feel of her in his arms.

I don't want to go, Lord. He swallowed, trying to stuff the emotion down so that he could get through the goodbye.

She pulled back. "I'm going to miss you," she whispered.

"So am I, darlin'."

Her eyes watered up at the endearment. "Call me every day?"

"I will."

"Text?"

"Of course."

"The boys wanted to know if they could write you."

"Definitely." He grinned at the thought. After all the years in the military, he finally had someone, other than his Pop and Gram, who wanted to write. "Let them know I'll write back as soon as I get a letter."

She leaned forward and touched her forehead to his. "Are you sure you have to leave right now?"

No! He wanted to change his mind and stay, but he had loose ends to tie up. "I need to say goodbye to my Gram before I head back to the fort."

She sighed. "I know. Just wished…"

"Me too."

"Hurry back to me."

"I will."

He slipped his arms around her and kissed her, pouring out every unspoken emotion. Leaving no doubt in her mind how much he cared and that she would be the only one in his thoughts.

When he broke off the kiss, a tear slid down her cheek. "Don't cry, darlin'."

She nodded and wiped the tears away. "Drive carefully. Let me know when you make it to your stops. 'Kay?"

"All right." He stepped back, still holding her hand.

"Go before I break down."

He let her hand go, hating that he had to. On an inhale, he whirled around. *Don't look back, Robinson. It'll only hurt worse.* His strides ate up the distance to his Harley.

The roar of his bike didn't drown out the pounding in his ears. Didn't even combat the pain in his chest while it split in two.

Lord, please get me back to her as soon as possible.

Each mile widened the gap as his heart headed farther south. He didn't understand why he was so upset. In two months, he'd be back in Maple Run and around the woman of his dreams.

Life wouldn't be perfect, it never was, but it would be as close as possible.

So why the anxiety coiling in his gut? He'd see her again. Call her every day like he promised. *Shake it off, Robinson.* A groan ripped from his lips, muffled by the sound of the wind and his Harley.

Lord, help me focus on You. You've guided me every step of the way. Please let the next two months fly by. Amen.

Delaney felt so foolish. Fear of rejection had kept her mute, and now Luke had no clue as to how she felt. It seemed ridiculous to be so upset, especially when she would see him again.

Yet, the innermost part of her brain wouldn't stop chiding her. She should have said "I love you" instead of watching him ride away. Far, far away.

A glance at her cell phone clock told her he was probably out of the state of Virginia. Was he supposed to stop in Tennessee? She had no idea how long people on motorcycles traveled.

Plus, it was just him.

If he had to travel with kids, he probably would have stopped already.

She laid her head against the breakroom table. If he would just call her and put her out of her misery, she could function.

The door opened, the creak making her ears twitch in complaint.

"You all right, Dee?"

She looked up into Dwight's worried face. He had another couple of weeks in the cast, but he was finally less grumpy. "I'm okay."

He raised an eyebrow. "Really? Or are you just saying that."

"Okay," she sighed. "I'm miserable. I wish he didn't have to leave."

Dwight sat down next to her. "So, big sis, anything you want to talk about? You seem awfully cozy with Luke."

She stared at him. "Are you really trying to go the protective brother route?"

"When have I not?"

Good point. "I think God's giving me a second chance, D."

Dwight smiled. "I'm happy for you."

"Really? No objection? No telling me I'm going too fast?"

"You've been talking to Mama, huh?"

"Maybe."

"Dee, when it comes down to it, only you and God know what's right in your life. We can offer our opinions, and you *know* Mama will. However, don't let that influence your decision. We aren't you, and we don't have to live with your choices." He pointed a finger at her. "You do."

"But how do I know the right one to make?" *Like withholding a declaration of love?*

"Prayer. Lots and lots of prayer."

She nodded. It was something she hadn't done a lot of. Sure, she talked to God on a daily basis. Sometimes hourly depending on how the day was going, but those felt more like moments of her talking at Him, not *to* Him.

"What did you pray when you were trying to decide if your relationship with Nina was the right thing?"

He sat back in the chair, crossing his legs in front of him. "I wanted to make sure that I was hearing God right. Plus, I wanted to be the man she deserved."

"Aw, Dwight, that's the sweetest thing I've ever heard you say."

He chuckled, ducking his head. "What can I say?" He shrugged. "She made me want to be worthy of her love."

"Oh, lil' brother." Dee held a hand over her heart. "You two are beautiful together. It took me awhile to see that. It's the baggage. It surrounds me, drags me down."

"Everyone has baggage."

"I'm a widow with two kids. My baggage doesn't look like others'."

"Does Luke have a problem with that?"

"No." She drew the word out, then placed her head in her hands. Even though they discussed kids, she never asked him what he wanted. Luke had been concerned about her feelings, not the other way around.

Dwight tugged on her arm. "You don't have to figure out everything today, but you should ask yourself and God so that you do know."

"He asked me if I wanted more kids." She peered at Dwight through the cracks between her fingers. "*But* I never asked him if he wanted any. See, he's already better at this relationship than I am. I can't do this, D."

Dwight took her face in his hands. "Sis, it's not a race. It's a partnership and the beauty is that there are things he's going to be better at. You want that, because when life gets hectic and starts throwing curve balls at you, you'll need someone to divvy up the work. Look at how he stepped in to help cook here. Not everyone would or could do that. It doesn't make you a failure to have different priorities."

She nodded.

"But, don't forget to treat him with the same care he shows you."

"Are we switching birth roles? You're the oldest now?"

Dwight chuckled. "No, but I'm the wisest." He winked when she rolled her eyes.

"No, I'm pretty sure old sums it up."

"We're the same age."

"Not mentally."

"Hey," he said spreading his hands. "One day you'll arrive at my level. Until then, I promise not to look down at you."

"Oh, you." She shoved him.

"It's time for me to go make sure my wife comes home." Dwight stood up. "She's been staring at the ledger longer than usual.

"Everything okay?" A brief wave of panic filtered through.

"Everything's fine. She's a touch of a perfectionist. Wants to figure out how to make the profits even better."

Whew. Her shoulders dropped. "Tell her to relax. We're good. Thankful even. Tell her to go home to her husband and kids."

"That's why she wants to make more profits."

"Why?" Her brow wrinkled.

"She's pregnant."

"Oh my goodness!" She stood up and hugged him. "Congratulations. When is she due?"

"End of March."

"A spring baby! I love it." She couldn't stop grinning.

Nina wanted a family more than anything, and God was blessing her with it. She couldn't be happier for the two of them. "You nervous?"

"Nah. What could be harder than twins?"

"Triplets?" She laughed.

Dwight shuddered and pointed a finger at her. "Don't even."

"What? You asked."

He shook his head. "I'm leaving before you suck this conversation in the wrong direction."

"Love you too, Brother."

"Who doesn't?"

Dee shook her head then bowed to pray.

Thank you for giving me a brother who knows how to make me laugh and take my mind off my own troubles. I pray that You would bless them with a healthy baby. Please let this pregnancy go smoothly for Nina.

She paused thinking of her Texan soldier. *And Lord, please help me be deserving of Luke. Help me to respect and care for him as he cares for me. In Jesus' Name, Amen.*

Chapter Nineteen

"Crusoe, Colonel wants to see you."

Luke nodded at Banks, then stood up from his cubicle. Since he turned in his separation paperwork, he knew a talk from the Colonel was coming.

Even though he gave him a heads up, a longer talk was bound to ensue. The Colonel wouldn't be himself if he didn't try and persuade Luke to stay. He knocked on the door, waiting for the command to enter.

"Come in."

Before Luke could go to attention, Colonel Rhodes was already barking. "At ease, Sergeant First Class." The Colonel pointed to one of the blue chairs situated in front of his oak desk. "Have a seat."

"Thank you, sir."

The Colonel folded his arms on his desk. Framed awards covered the walls and a coin collection sat prominently on his desktop. "Why do you want to separate? You're one of our best NCOs."

Truth or work around? "I met a girl."

"I see. She doesn't want to be a military wife?"

"Been there, done that, got the folded flag." He winced. He didn't mean to sound so callous.

Colonel Rhodes' eyebrows rose. The thin white lines stood out against his weathered face. "Daunting task there, Crusoe."

"She's worth it, sir."

"Anyone I know, by chance?"

Heat claimed his face. "Jones's widow, sir."

"You kidding me?"

Luke shook his head.

"You went to make amends with her too?"

At his nod, the Colonel scoffed.

"You finally done punishing yourself?"

Finally. After all the years of beating himself, he was finally accepting the Lord's olive branch. "Yes, sir."

Colonel Rhodes leaned back, his hands folded over his stomach. "This certainly is an interesting development. I suppose you're not going to like what I have to say." He snorted. "Most likely Mrs. Jones won't either."

Unease curled around him like heavy smoke. "What is it, sir?"

"We need you to deploy before you separate."

Silence filled the air.

He blinked.

Inhaled.

Exhaled. "She's going to flip," he whispered.

"She just might, Crusoe." Colonel Hayes nodded sympathetically. "It's only for a month. Gives you time to come back and out-process. They need an expert to train some guys and your number was up."

Luke sat there, too stunned to do anything else. What he wanted to do, or even say, he couldn't. The Army frowned upon men who bemoaned their fate.

Seriously though, two months away from separation and they wanted him to deploy? It seemed a waste of

funds and a major inconvenience. "When do I leave?"
And how am I going to tell Delaney?
"Next week."
So soon? "I'll get ready."
"I know you will. Be careful out there, Crusoe. She doesn't need two flags."
He closed his eyes at the insensitive remark. "Dismissed."
Luke walked out and glanced at the wall clock. It was late enough he could take a lunch, but what he really needed to do was call Delaney. Or maybe he should FaceTime with her. He groaned.
Lord, why? I can't tell her I'm deploying one last time. She'll freak out.
Then again, he couldn't blame her.
He headed outside and got in his truck. It was a good thing he drove it instead of his Harley.
Now he could have some privacy to use the video chat settings to talk to Delaney. He opened his text messages, tapping on the last message to her. He wrote a new one:
Hey, can you talk? FaceTime?
He waited for her reply.
Sure can. Give me a sec.
Soon the ringing from the app took over the screen. He pressed the talk button and Delaney's chocolate eyes drew him in.
"Look at you, all handsome in uniform."
He shook his head to hide his embarrassment. "Hey, darlin'." Her face practically sparkled in her light blue shirt.
"You going to lunch?"
"Yes."
"What's wrong?" Her eyes darkened with concern. "Usually you'd be talking my ear off by now."

"You got a problem with how much I talk?"

"Luke..."

He sighed. "I turned in my separation paperwork yesterday."

"Okay." She waited, and he knew she could tell a "but" was coming.

"They want me to deploy one last time."

Delaney's eyes filled with tears.

"Darlin', please don't cry." An ache filled his heart.

Maybe their relationship wasn't such a good idea. He never wanted to cause her pain, but life forced his hand.

"When do you leave?" The choked whisper punched him in the gut.

"Next week."

A tear slipped down her face.

This was the worst idea he ever had.

If he told her over the phone, without the aid of video, he'd knew she'd cry but wouldn't have to see it. This...this was tearing him apart. He intended it to be a reassuring factor, but watching her heart break in front of him wasn't comforting for either one of them.

"I'm so sorry, Delaney."

"You couldn't help it. They never give you a choice." The words sounded bitter.

"Still."

She shook her head, bolstering herself. "No, I told you I could handle it, so that's what I'll do." She offered him a smile but the strain was evident around her mouth and eyes.

"It's only a month."

"Thank God."

"I'll write. Email. Call when I can."

"I know you will. And I'll do the same."

"I'll call you later tonight."

"Wait." She paused, biting her lip. "There's something I wanted to tell you. I didn't say anything at first because I thought it was too soon, but I don't want you to deploy without knowing."

Finally! That was all the prompting he needed. "I know how much you love me, Delaney. I love you, too."

"Luke," she whispered. Tears slipped down her face. "You're so good to me."

"You deserve it."

"I love you so much."

"I love you, too. We're going to get through this. Okay?"

She nodded, wiping the last remnants of tears away.

"I don't want you worrying about me. God's brought us this far."

"You're right."

He winked. "Of course." *And he could only pray he'd continue to be right.*

As soon as the screen faded to black, Dee let the sobs out. They wracked her body with a fierceness that should have scared her if she were in her right mind.

How could God do this to her? He knew how she felt about the military…about deployments. Yet, He was sending Luke off on one last hoorah.

It was like a bad scene from a drama movie. Everyone knew what happened in those movies. The hero never came back.

"Delaney? What on earth?"

Her mother's voice broke through the sobs that shook her frame. The bed dipped and her mother's arms came around her.

"Delaney, this is a bad sense of déjà vu you're giving me. Calm down and tell me what's wrong."

She tried to speak, but more cries escaped.

"Does it have something to do with Luke?"

She nodded, trying to catch her breath.

"Is he...dead?"

"No, Ma. Why would you say that?" Her breath kick started as indignation ran through her body. It was bad enough he had to deploy, and now her mother was asking ridiculous questions.

Her tears dried up as resentment took hold.

"Girl, you're over here crying and boohooing like the world is coming to an end. What else am I supposed to think?"

"He's deploying."

"I thought you decided you could handle his job?" Her mother's mouth tilted to the side in confusion, her arms folded across her chest.

"That was before he told me he was separating and getting a job out here."

A look of shock took place on her mother's face. "He is?"

She nodded. "Except they want him to deploy one last time before he gets out." A shiver went up her spine. "Oh, Ma, you know what that means?"

"No, I don't. What does it mean?"

"People never come back when they're supposed to."

"Delaney Jane, are you God?"

"No." *Great, just what she needed, a lecture instead of sympathy.*

"Then stop acting like you can see into the future. You have no reason, other than your warped way of thinking, to believe that man ain't coming back to you.

Maybe God's trying to make you see how little your faith really is."

She inhaled sharply. "That's harsh, Ma."

"No, that's truth, Delaney." Her mother stood, placing her hands on her hips. "I wouldn't be a good parent if I didn't point out your flaws. And baby girl, you have a major one going on right now.

Faith is the substance of things hoped for, the evidence of things *not* seen, Delaney Jane. Stop trying to see your future and trust in a God who knows the future."

"How? My mind keeps telling me what happened last time. Playing that scene over and over when the Major came with the chaplain. I can't go through that again."

"Perhaps God knows that and has provided a way so you won't have to go through that again. Trust Him, Delaney. *Trust Him.*"

Her heart hurt, but the words her mother admonished her with hurt more. She never thought of herself as lacking trust.

Okay, perhaps a time or two, but she thought she repented of it and cleared it away.

Why was it still bogging her down?

"I'll try."

"Don't try, Delaney. Do." Her mother strolled to her door but stopped, turning back. "And you need to remember your boys are here. We can't have you scaring them over something like this. Gather your courage, because when you tell them where Luke's going, they'll need your strength."

Ouch. How was she going to tell them this? "You're right," she sighed.

Her mother dipped her head in exasperation. "In the meantime, I suggest you open up a Bible."

Feeling appropriately chastised, Delaney grabbed her Bible off her nightstand. When was the last time she opened it? A wave of embarrassment flew through her. "I'm sorry, Lord."

She sighed and opened the Bible. Since her mother harped about her lack of trust, maybe that's where she needed to focus. She looked in the concordance and found a corresponding scripture in Proverbs.

"Trust in the Lord with all thine heart; and lean not unto thine own understanding. In all thy ways acknowledge him, and he shall direct thy paths."

That's what she'd been doing. Looking at Luke's deployment through her own understanding.

Lord, how am I supposed to look at it? Circumstances taught me what happens when a man I love deploys.

She reread the scripture. "Okay, so it says to acknowledge You. How? I know You're God. Is that acknowledgment?" She bit her lip. "Okay, here goes. I acknowledge You, Lord. I acknowledge that You are my Savior. My Maker. The One who rules all."

Rules all.

Didn't that include Luke's deployment?

The deployment was no surprise to God, no matter how much it felt like she was hit by a Mack truck. And her response certainly wasn't a surprise to God.

Even her relationship with Luke wasn't a surprise. Nothing was a surprise yet she was acting like it was. Because, to her, it was.

Which was probably why the Bible cautioned against leaning on one's own understanding. Her vision, her view of life, wasn't wide or comprehensive enough to get her through life's trials and tribulations.

"That's why You want us to lean on You. Because we don't know what's going to happen."

She closed her eyes. Trust was so difficult. It was like stepping off a ledge and praying there would be a net to catch her. She shook her head. No. With God, there was a reassurance that there would be a net.

He was her net.

He wouldn't let life defeat her. There were countless Scriptures in the Bible that confirmed that.

Her mother was right. She had little faith *and* trust, allowing her mind to spin out of control and set her on a path of worry.

No matter what happened, God would see her through. He knew how she felt about deployments. Knew how she felt about Luke.

It was up to her to remind herself and shush the enemy who wanted to continuously point out the outcome of Parker's deployment.

She had no idea why God took Parker and might never know. But she couldn't forget the peace of coming to grips with her new reality.

Now she needed to make peace with her current circumstances.

I trust You, Lord. Right here. Right now. I make a commitment to trust You and lean on You and fill my mind with Your truth. Please give me the faith necessary to get through Luke's deployment.

"In Jesus' Name, Amen."

Chapter Twenty

Luke stretched out on his bed, his mail pile lying next to him. Even though Delaney emailed him daily, she had sent a letter as well. So did Preston and Philip.

The corners of his mouth turned up as warmth spread through his heart. He opened Philip's first.

Philip reminded him of himself as a kid. The boy was a little reserved, but he wore his heart on his sleeve.

When they said good-bye back in Maple Run, he thought Philip would cry. He'd stooped down to look him in the eye and remind him that he was coming back.

"Thanks for being my buddy, Philip."

"'Welcome, Mr. Luke."

"I'll be back, okay?"

Philip looked him in the eyes. "Promise?"

"Promise."

He unfolded the letter as the memory faded.

Dear Mr. Luke,

I hope it's not too hot overseas. Mama says you're probably melting because it's a lot hotter over there than in Virginia. Is that true? Because it's real hot here. We've been going to the pool every day to keep cool. As soon as we get out

of the water, we get hot again. I can't imagine any place being hotter than Virginia.
Anyway, I hope you're doing good. And I didn't forget what you told me. I haven't told anyone else, not even Pres.
Your friend,
Philip

Luke smiled. He promised Philip that when he came back, he'd ask Delaney to marry him. Philip had assured him he could keep a secret. The boy had promised with a solemnity that had touched his heart.

He pulled out Preston's envelope and opened it. Stuff fell out, spreading over his stomach. He picked a piece up and laughed out loud. Ninja Turtle stickers.

Hi Mr. Luke,
When are you coming back? Mom said you're only supposed to be gone for a month but she keeps staring at the calendar so I don't trust her. Parents can be sneaky. Since you're not my dad, I figured you'll tell me the truth. But if you wanted to be my dad, that would be cool. Just don't be sneaky.

He laughed out loud. The kid was a trip.

I think if you decide to marry my Mom you should buy her a ring. Apparently, girls like that kind of thing. I think a dog would be a better gift, but she may not like that. So if you decide to get a dog instead, you can give him to me and Philip. We'll take care of him. I even have some names picked out.
Our neighbor has a Goldendoodle, and I think that's an awful name for a dog so please don't get that.
Always (why do people write that anyway),
Preston

When his laughter subsided, he grabbed the notepad from his nightstand. He was going to have to look up dogs and check with Delaney to see if it was okay to get one.

Boys should have a pet, and the twins were responsible enough to watch over one. If one discounted the state of their room and family basement.

No goldendoodles. He set the notepad aside and grabbed the last letter.

Delaney.

For a brief moment, he wondered if she had written to Parker. *Of course, she did.* He'd never felt jealous of Jones until this moment. Knowing it wasn't the first time she'd written to a soldier.

Then reality set in.

How much harder was this for her since Jones died?

Shame set in. *Lord, please let me return safely to her so it's the last time she has to do this.* He opened the letter. It smelled of sunshine and strawberries, just like her.

Luke,

I have no earthly idea what to write. It seems like there's not enough words or paper to tell you how I feel. I'll start by telling you I love you, and I'm so glad you love me. It would suck royally to be in this alone.

Laughter escaped his lips.

Since you've been gone, I've raided my fridge nightly for a piece of dessert. I hope you aren't expecting me to be the same size as when you left.

Her metabolism was off the charts. There was no physical evidence that she had two kids or liked to eat desserts. He'd be surprised if she gained a pound.

Then again, the boys are running me ragged. I can't wait for school to start again. Does that make me a bad mom for saying so? They were excited to write you and refused to let me read over their shoulders. I have no idea if their penmanship is even legible.

Also, I got an unexpected phone call yesterday. A woman named Rosa Robinson called.

He groaned. His grandmother had called? Luke wasn't sure if he wanted to continue the letter. What could have possessed his grandmother to call Delaney?

She's an absolute sweetheart. We may have traded a recipe or two. I can smell the snickerdoodles even now.

"No fair," he whispered.

I would have included them in the letter, but the boys discovered them and they're all gone. Lol, just joking. The package will either beat the letter or come right behind it.

"Yes!" He was going to be in snickerdoodle heaven soon.

Well, that's all for now. Unlike me, my mother has no qualms about reading over my shoulder. I'll save the mushy stuff for the email.

Love,
Delaney

A full grin stretched across his lips. *Lord, I want to marry that woman.* He was convinced it was the only way to live the rest of his life, with her by his side in the quaint town of Maple Run.

Funny, he never even considered asking her to move to Texas.

When he drove back home, the first thing he'd done was tell his father how he felt about Delaney. His Pop wasn't surprised.

"Son, I could hear it in your voice."

"Really?" He rocked back on his boots.

"Yep. The love of a good woman changes a man, clear through to the way he speaks to everyone else. Even your Gram noticed it."

That's because the woman watched him like a hawk. He knew it was out of love, but growing up, it had been disconcerting to a teenage boy.

"I'm planning on getting a job up there, Pop."

"I figured as much. You be sure to bring her down here and visit."

His stomach tightened. Part of him instinctively knew his father wouldn't uproot. Texas was in his blood. "Of course we will. And you visit, too."

"Will be up there for Thanksgiving."

And that had been the end of the conversation. His father and grandmother weren't going to move. He was just going to have to be okay with seeing them on the holidays.

It really wasn't that much different than what he did now, thanks to the Army. He could only pray they would love Delaney and the boys as much as he did.

Life went on and it sucked. Delaney wanted to shout at everyone. Make them slow down or at least allow her the time to bemoan the fact that she didn't have Luke around to brighten her days.

Instead, she continued to serve at The Pit and spend time with her boys—and really, how could she begrudge them that?

Yet, when nighttime came, her heart ached. Darkness seemed to lurk in the corners of her bedroom. Part of her wanted to call out and ask the boys to come in for a sleep over.

Only they were too big for that, and she wouldn't survive a night of feet and fists in her face. She'd watched them sleep before: comical and mind blowing all at once.

No, she had to figure out how to deal with the quiet and the shadows that begged her to remember her past and why being with Luke was wrecking her peace of mind.

Worrying for Luke's safety had her jumping at every phone call and knock on the door. Every time she felt it press in, she talked to God about it. She became intent on mastering trust. Unfortunately, she realized trusting the Lord wasn't a lifetime-achievement skill, more like a minute-by-minute success.

So far, the longest she'd gone without worry gnawing at her bones was a half hour.

That was due to preoccupation. She had read a bedtime story to the boys after overseeing their nighttime rituals of brushing teeth and saying prayers. She smiled softly as she remembered Preston's words.

"Dear Heavenly Father. Could you bring Mr. Luke back? Mama's going to go crazy waiting for him. She thinks we don't notice, but we do. In Jesus' Name, Amen."

Delaney had been torn between laughter and tears over the sweetness of Preston's prayer. Now, that she was settling down with her Bible and some quiet time, her mind was starting to spin out of control once again.

Lord, please bring peace to me. I hate that the boys know I'm slowly going crazy with worry. What is that teaching them? Better yet, what does that say about me? I don't want to doubt, but it feels so overwhelming. Please help my unbelief and help me to trust in You.

The words flew freely.

She paused to listen for God's response. That was another thing she'd been working on: listening. Before, she had been content with zipping a prayer heavenward and pressing forward.

Now, she was taking the time to be quiet and listen for His still, small voice. It wasn't easy. Her mind was easily distracted, but she knew it would be worth it.

She sat there until sweet peace enveloped her like a hug. It wasn't a word, but it felt like a response from God. *Thank You.* Delaney grabbed her Bible to read a chapter before letting sleep succumb.

Abraham's Faith Confirmed.

Of all the chapters to read. Funny how God used the Word to speak to her. What better way to drum the lesson of trust in. Abraham was told to sacrifice his son. The *promised* son.

She shuddered. What parent wanted to have to come to a point in their life where it was their child or God? Yet, Abraham did it. Trusted in the Lord with all his heart.

Why was it so easy for Abraham to do, and yet she was holding on to a man—not of her blood—tighter than a winning lottery ticket?

Even God sacrificed His Son. Sacrificed Jesus in hopes that one…just one person would find his way back into the fold. *You did all that and still I question. Doubt.*

Shame filled her heart. *I don't want to doubt, Lord. I surrender my hopes and dreams. I place Luke's safety in your very capable hands. The best place he can be. Please keep him safe. And thank You. Thank You for already providing for Luke's safety. I trust You.*

The words rang true in her heart. For now, in this still silent moment, she'd achieved trust. And that was good enough for the night. She placed her Bible on the nightstand just as her cell phone rang.

An unknown number filled the screen.

Luke.

"Hello?"

The operator connected the call.

"Luke?"

"Hey, darlin', how are you?"

"Great, now that I get to hear your voice." She leaned back on her pillow, warmth filling her soul. "How are you?"

"Better now. I got your letter."

"Did you get the cookies yet?"

"No, I didn't. Did Gram really call you?"

She chuckled. "She did. Apparently, *someone* forgot to send her a recipe and her curiosity won out. So, she called and we traded a couple of recipes."

"Maple Pit ones?"

"Nah, my mother would skin me alive. Just family ones we use around the house."

"Gram's probably happy as a hog in some slop."

"Your country roots are showing."

"But you love me anyway."

"I sure do." It filled her soul, making time stand still. This conversation was a reminder of why she decided he was worth it, regardless of his job.

No one else could put a smile on her face, warm her heart, and spike her pulse with a few quick low timbre words.

"Five minutes," the operator broke through.

Delaney closed her eyes, willing the tears away. "Have you looked for any places to live?"

"I have. Y'all don't have a lot of apartments popping up there."

She chuckled. "True. I can see if there's a vacancy in Dwight's old building." Move in with me, she wanted to shout. But in order for that to happen, she needed a proposal and a ring.

Well, and a marriage certificate. Time sure did inch along at times.

"Thanks, Delaney. I'm going to go, before they cut us off."

"Love you, Luke."

"Love you, too, darlin'. Sweet dreams."

Chapter Twenty-one

If life were a movie, the weather would be an indicator that the path he was currently on was coming up to a pivotal moment.

After all, his first date with Delaney had been filled with abundant sunshine and an idyllic atmosphere. It would be forever cemented in his mind.

However, today, the precarious situation he found himself in belied the repetitive setting.

Just like yesterday, the day before, and the day before that, the sun blazed while sweat trailed down every nook and cranny his uniform and Kevlar vest would allow.

His men ribbed one another good naturedly as they prepared to board the helo. Despite being thousands of miles away from home and those he loved, it was an okay day.

One step closer to returning home.

He waited until everyone was aboard before taking a seat. The guys knew that today wasn't a game. All they learned cumulated up to this point. His eyes scanned the horizon and took in the jagged mountains that rose in the desert.

His shades shielded his eyes from the bright sun as they continued their search.

A warning sounded from the helicopter. Deafening in its alert.

Panic filled his being.

Shouts filled the comms.

His eyes searched for the cause of the warning, but it was too late. The helo jerked and he slammed into the wall, pain searing up his right side.

The aircraft began to spin out of control, tossing him around.

No! This wasn't how it was supposed to be. He was supposed to return to Delaney, healthy and ready to love her for the rest of his life.

Only now, it seemed that he would never have the chance.

Lord God, don't let me return in a coffin. Don't let her get another folded up flag.

It was his last thought before the darkness devoured him.

The doorbell pealed through the air. Delaney glanced at her nightstand, checking the time. *7:00pm.* She stood up and stretched. It was probably Nina coming by to keep her company.

Ever since Luke left, someone in the family took it upon himself or herself to keep Delaney's mind occupied. Still, her heart ached from the pain of missing him.

At least she and Nina were growing close in the process.

The doorbell rang again, breaking through her musings.

"Mom, doorbell!" Preston yelled.

"Got it!" she shouted as she hustled past the boys' room and down the stairs. She slowed as she rounded the stairwell to answer the door. A memory of Dwight's warning sounded in her head.

Just because we live in a small town doesn't mean you shouldn't be cautious.

She walked up to the peephole to peer through. Two men stood outside.

She froze. "No, no, no," she mumbled. Her body struggled to suck in air as panic clawed her throat, filled it with an ache of emotion. This could *not* be happening.

She glanced at the doorknob as if it were a serpent. Could she do this again? Have her heart ripped out again?

The doorbell rang again and she jumped.

Lord, please!

Her hand clapped over her mouth, stifling a sob, but refusing to answer the door wasn't going to change anything. Unless they had the wrong house, her world was about to be torn apart. She reached for the door and opened it.

Micah.

Luke's friend and an older gentleman, decked out in his uniform, stood on her front porch. Her stomach rolled as her dinner threatened to reverse tracks. She folded her arms, pinching the skin in the inside of her elbow.

Ow. Why couldn't this be a dream? "Is he…?" Her voice came out warbled as tears spilled down her cheeks.

"He's alive, Delaney."

The air left her body and she sagged against the door. *Thank You, God.* Movement entered her periphery, as her mind tried to grasp Micah stepping into the house.

"Let's go inside so we can talk." His voice was calm, hands steady.

She nodded numbly. "Do you want something to drink?" Odd how flat her voice sounded.

"No, sit, Delaney." Micah motioned to the other gentleman. "This is Chaplain Foster."

"Chaplain." She met Micah's gaze as she settled onto the couch. Why was it always the living room where life was ruined? "Just tell me."

Micah licked his lips. "Rocket-Propelled-Grenade."

"Oh, God," she covered her face. *Please, Lord, don't do this to me.*

"He survived. He's not dead, Delaney."

She looked up. "There's a 'but.'" *There always was a "but."* The silence in between his words screamed there was a missing piece. "What is it?"

He hung his head, his bald head reflecting the ceiling light. His voice came out hoarse. "There's still a chance he might not make it."

"No, no, no!" *Why?!* The cry rent through her mind as tears continued to flood her face.

"Ms. Jones." The Chaplain sat next to her, placing a hand on her arm. "Luke was coherent when they took him to the hospital. He specifically asked for Micah to accompany me to talk to you. His utmost concern was you."

It was just like Luke to worry about her. She shook her head. From the moment he expressed his interest, he'd done his best to make sure she could handle his job. Handle the military way of life. She faced the Chaplain.

"Can I see him?"

Finding Love

"I'm sorry, Ms. Jones," the Chaplain stated. "You need base access, and since you two aren't married, I can't authorize that." Regret pulled his features down, emphasizing the crow's feet and the lines around his mouth.

Instead of seeing kindness and misery, she saw stubbornness and a wall. The tilt of her chin stuck out before she could stop it.

"Well, it's a good thing my survivor's benefits grants me base access. I guess there is a perk to having your husband *die* for his country." Fury swirled around her like a F-5 tornado.

The Chaplain's eyes widened in shock.

"Calm down, Delaney." Micah spoke soothingly, holding a hand up in plea. "I forgot to tell the Chaplain that part." He nodded toward the Chaplain. "We'll get you there. You'll see Luke soon."

The anger left her at his statement. It wasn't the Chaplain's fault that her insides were churning, causing her perfectly calm façade to change in a split second. All she could think of was the hurt Luke must be in.

"What's wrong with him?"

"Internal injuries. They wouldn't divulge a lot. Think they're waiting to hear from you."

She nodded, licking her lips, wondering why her voice was so dry. "I need to call my mother."

Micah nodded in understanding. She took her cell out of her pocket. There was no way to soften the news. She didn't have time for that. She needed to be on the first flight out of Virginia and on her way to Luke.

"Delaney, it's kind of busy here tonight. Can I call you back?"

"Sorry, Ma, but Luke's friend and a chaplain are here. Luke's been hurt." The words wrenched out as the horror hit her over again.

"Not again," her mother whispered.

"He's alive, but they're not sure if he's going to make it. I need to go see him."

"Of course."

Dwight's voice sounded in the background, and she heard her mother explain what happened.

"Dee?"

"Dwight," she sobbed out.

"He's going to be fine, DeeDee. I'm sending Nina over to watch the boys, all right?"

"Thanks, Dwight."

"We'll be praying for him."

The next few hours flew by as she packed and headed for the airport. Micah agreed to escort her to Germany where Luke was. They wanted to move him stateside but had to stabilize him first.

She'd never been so grateful to already own a passport. Who knew she would need it to fly over the Atlantic in a moment's notice? *Lord, please don't let me fly over there only to say good-bye. Please, please heal him here on this Earth. Please, God.*

♡

"Robinson, you need to wake up. Robinson, come on, soldier."

The incessant noise aggravated the pain in his head. Why did people feel the need to talk so loud when you were laid up in the hospital? At least, he hoped it was a hospital.

Surely, God wouldn't have to wake him up in heaven.

He told his eyes to open—but nothing.

"Come on, soldier. Open those eyes."

I'm trying. He really was, but his brain refused to cooperate. Did that mean something was wrong? A relentless beeping noise picked up speed, making the pain in his head worse. Why, oh why, couldn't they shut that off?

"Turn that off."

A wave of pain crushed his skull at the order. It was probably said in a normal tone, but it sounded like a cymbal in his noggin.

"Robinson, if you can hear me, you need to know you're in the hospital. We'll take good care of you, soldier. Hang in there."

Thank God. He needed to get back to Maple Run. Back to Delaney and the boys so that he could spend the rest of his days relaxing. He may even decide to take up a permanent apron at The Pit.

The thought of jumping out of perfectly sound aircraft had lost its appeal.

The plane ride was too quiet, as if the passengers knew the severity of her situation. Delaney took a deep breath, continuing her constant state of prayer.

So far, she'd momentarily stopped to say "yes" or "no" to the flight attendants' questions.

Every time the fear gripped her, she repeated Scripture hoping it would calm her heart and ease her fears. It was rough.

Her mind wouldn't let her forget that she'd lost Parker to a helicopter crash. She had always been thankful he died instantly. The thought of her husband being in pain was too much to bear.

Only now, her thoughts were full of Luke and the pain he must be going through. It fueled her prayers as her heart threatened to break. Yet, if he was hurting, he was alive.

It was a somewhat irrational line of thought, but she needed all the hope she could get. When he had told her he was going to deploy for a month, fear had gripped her then.

The old uncertainty raised its head. It was one thing to think he was going back to the military to finish his career before retiring. It was something else knowing he had to deploy.

The memory of Phillip's and Preston's reactions pressed against her. Threatened to unleash—something stronger, like the tears that had been trying to fall since she boarded the plane.

To say they had been traumatized was an understatement.

Preston was almost inconsolable. She didn't want to promise him Luke would be okay, but her heart urged her to say whatever she could to get his tears and pain to stop.

"Pres, I'm going to get him and bring him home. We'll take good care of him."

"What if…what if," he hiccupped. "What if it's too late?" The wail that broke free was enough to break her heart.

"Pray, Pres. Pray with all your might that it's not. I'll call as soon as I know how he is. Okay?"

He clung to her so tight, she couldn't breathe. Philip had been more subdued, as was his way, but his tears no less powerful.

When she walked out her house, they had formed a circle with Nina to pray for Luke.

With haste, she unbuckled her seatbelt, racing down the aisle to make it before she lost what little food she'd eaten.

Chapter Twenty-two

"Luke?"

A soft whisper caressed his face, and a warm hand touched his cheek. He snuggled deeper, embracing the dream where Delaney's presence washed over him.

Perhaps being knocked unconscious wasn't such a bad thing.

"Sweetheart, wake up."

His brow wrinkled. The whisper was a little louder and felt more real than his dream. He begged his eyes to open, so that he could figure out what was going on.

Why did he smell sunshine and strawberries? Why did it feel like Delaney was caressing his face?

For the first time in who knew how long, Luke opened his eyes.

Delaney!

She was here. In person. Not a dream or a figment of his imagination, but flesh and blood. He wanted to gaze at her forever, but the light was blinding. His eyes slid closed.

"You're here." His voice sounded as rough as sandpaper.

He opened his eyes again just as tears filled Delaney's eyes. "And so are you."

Instinctively, he tried to reach for her with his right arm, but pain shot up it and a groan slipped out. *Was it broken?*

"Hey, it's okay." She ran her hand over his head. "Relax. Don't try to move, okay?"

"All right," he rasped. Licked his lips. "Can I get some water?"

"No, but the nurse left ice chips in case you woke up." She placed a chip in his mouth.

The chip was cool, refreshing his tongue and quickly melting into nothingness. "More please." The next one felt better than the last. "Thank you so much, darlin'."

"Of course. How are you feeling?"

"Like I fell out of a perfectly good aircraft." He tried to laugh, but the pain was intense.

"Let me call the nurse." Wrinkles marred her forehead, worry darkening her beautiful eyes.

"No, wait."

Delaney paused, her hand hovering over the call button.

"Just let me look at you. I heard you in my dream...thought *you* were a dream."

Her hair fell in soft waves, and she wore the yellow dress from their date. Emotion clogged his throat. "I was afraid I wouldn't see you again."

"Me too."

"Can't believe you came all the way out here."

"Of course I did. I had to be sure you would make it." She found his hand and gave it a slight squeeze. "Needed to see it with my own two eyes."

"I'm all right." But he couldn't say it without wincing.

She leaned forward and kissed his forehead. "Can I please call the doctor now? You look like you're in pain."

"All right." All he wanted to do was stare at her.

Then again, he could do that regardless if the doctor was in the room or not. He thought for sure his days were numbered when the warning sounded loud and clear.

Thank You, Lord, for my life. And thank You so much for not ending my life for Delaney's sake.

Even though he wanted a chance to live, dying would have been easy on his part. Awakening in heaven with a pure body wasn't a hardship.

No, it was the thought of what his death would do to Delaney that helped him cling to life. Judging by the look on her face, the victory wasn't clearly established.

A knock signaled on the door and a doctor appeared in his line of sight.

"Sergeant First Class Robinson, we sure are glad to see you awake, soldier."

He dipped his head slightly, biting back a groan in regret. The pounding in his head made him want to lose his lunch—if he had any. "Thank you, Major."

The doctor leaned against the foot of the hospital bed. "I'm Major Hayes. I'd like to talk to you about your injuries."

Delaney tightened her grip. He caressed it with his thumb, trying to offer comfort.

"Go ahead."

"You broke your right leg in a couple of places when you landed. Your right arm, in case you haven't noticed, is also broken. That was an easy set and it should heal without a problem. You also had some internal bleeding, so we had to remove your spleen."

That explained the fire in his stomach.

"It was touch-n-go for a moment there, but you pulled through the night. Your vitals have stabilized and labs are looking much better. Of course, the blood transfusion might have helped."

Good grief. How close to the end had he been? Though curiosity burned his gut, he refrained from asking. No way Delaney wanted to hear the answer to that.

"Now what, Major?"

"Now you recover. I'll leave instructions with the nurses. Please listen to them. They're not out to torture you but to get you home that much sooner."

With a wave, he was out.

Delaney sank into the chair next to him.

"I still can't believe you're here."

"Where else would I be, Luke Robinson?"

"Taking care of the boys?" he asked cautiously.

"They demanded I bring you back home so that we could all take care of you."

He grinned, then frowned. Apparently he had a split lip too. "Ow."

"Yeah, you're pretty banged up." She ran a hand through his hair. "But I'm just glad you're alive."

"Come here," he murmured.

He wished he could raise up on his own strength, but exhaustion weighed him down. Still, one sweet kiss from her lips, and he got a second wind.

"I missed that."

"Mm-hmm, me too," she whispered against his lips. "But I think you need your rest. We can kiss later."

"All right, I get the point."

She sat back down, holding his hand and stroking his hair with the other. In a matter of minutes, he was asleep again.

As Luke closed his eyes, hiding his beautiful ice blue eyes, relief flooded her soul. She'd been on edge since she walked into his hospital room and seen the damage done to his rugged six-foot-three frame.

The bruising on his face, split lip, and various scrapes on his skin had rocked her to her core. Not to mention the broken bones.

He'd been *so* close.

The doctor listed his injuries as if they had been minor complications. But she remembered the pale look on his face last night. The room's dim lighting did nothing to enhance his pallor. He looked near death's door.

Micah had tried to get her to check into the fort's hotel. Instead, she grabbed a Bible and tucked herself into the lounge chair in Luke's room. She prayed, read, and prayed some more.

By the time the sun peeked through the blinds, she was pretty sure God was tired of hearing from her.

It was only then, in the midst of her exhaustion that sleep had claimed her.

Thank You, Lord, for waking him up and getting him through the night. Thank You so much.

A tear slipped down her cheek as she thought of how close she'd been to losing him. To losing a chance at the love she so recently found in his arms.

How the man managed to sneak so intricately into her heart was beyond her, but she refused to question it anymore. Life was precious and time waited for no one.

It was time to dive all-in to their relationship. She wouldn't let fear paralyze her again. Wouldn't let a lack of trust spin her into useless worry. It had all been for naught.

Sure, he'd been injured to the point he needed a blood transfusion, but it could have easily been a freak accident on the home front. And who knew what the future held?

No more worrying, Delaney. She'd no longer think their relationship was going too fast. When you knew, you knew. Plus, God confirmed that Luke Robinson was her second chance at love.

She wouldn't ignore the Almighty's direction. Not when she'd hammered on His door with prayers for direction. Instead, she'd accept the sweet gift God offered.

Finding love for the second time.

She walked to the corner of his hospital room and reached for her cellphone, sitting on the window ledge. As soon as she came in last night, she'd plugged it in to charge.

Now, she wanted to let the kids know Luke had awakened. They had been sad when she told them last night he wasn't awake yet.

"Mom!"

Her heart melted at the sound of Philip's voice. "Hey, bud. How are you guys?"

"Who cares? How's Mr. Luke?"

"He woke up. I got to talk to him for a couple of minutes."

"Then he's going to be okay? Can I talk to him?"

"He's going to be fine, sweetie. The doctor said they'll help him heal so he can get home as soon as possible."

"Can I talk to him, Mom?"

She stared at Luke's sleeping form. "I'm sorry, sweetie, he's asleep again. He's probably going to sleep a lot until his body heals."

"All right." The hurt tone tore at her heart.

"I'll try and call you the next time he wakes. Wait a minute, what time is it there?" It was two o'clock in Germany. She hadn't even thought to check the time difference, just knew the boys would need to talk to her.

"Eight o'clock. Grandma's making waffles for Preston."

"What about you?"

"I don't want them, Mom. Just regular ol' pancakes are just fine."

She chuckled. "Put your brother on the phone."

"'Kay. Love you."

"Preston!" Philip shouted, ringing her ear drums.

What was it with kids that they never walked toward the person but yelled at the top of their lungs wherever they were?

It was no wonder people lost their hearing by the time they were ready for retirement.

"Hi, Ma. Is he awake? Is he okay? Can I talk to him?"

"Slow down, Pres. He's sleeping. He'll be okay."

"He's still asleep?!" A whine filled his voice.

"Getting injured makes a person tired, Pres. I told Philip already, but I'll try and call when he wakes."

"When can he come home?"

"As soon as the doctor lets him." She grimaced. "I forgot to ask."

"Oh, Mom, see why you need us there?"

Dee chuckled. "I'm lost without you, Pres."

"Don't I know it. Hold on, Grandma wants to talk."

"How is he, DeeDee?"

"Alive and on the mend."

"Praise Jesus."

"Amen." Tears filled her eyes and she snuck another look at her handsome soldier. She sniffed.

"How are you holding up?"

"Great, now that I got to talk to him. He woke up briefly for a few minutes. Sweetest sight ever."

"Well, you tell him The Pit crew's been praying, and we're glad he's on the mend."

"I will."

"And Delaney Jane…"

Was she in trouble again? Her mother was spitting out her first and middle name too much lately. "Yes, Ma?"

"You bring that young man home and accept the opportunity the good Lord's given you. Understood?"

A grin split her face. "Understood, Ma."

Epilogue

Luke rowed across the river, heading for the spot where they had their first date. The memory still brought a smile to his face. This woman captivated his heart, and he'd do anything for her.

He smiled at Delaney, wondering if she had a clue as to what he was up to. It didn't hurt that they'd been out here a few times. Surely, she wouldn't suspect this time was any different. But it was. It was time to propose.

Truthfully, he'd been ready to since the day she flew into his hospital room. He couldn't believe she'd flown halfway around the world to be with him. He closed his eyes, remembering her in the yellow dress.

How the scent of strawberries chased the antiseptic smell away. He never thought he would be okay with being so sappy and sentimental over a woman. Until he met Delaney Jones.

She deserved his best, and he was intent on giving it to her for the next fifty years…God willing.

All he needed was a "yes" to his question and the next chapter of his life would be set. The first for their life together.

He paused, letting his arm rest and give his right leg a chance to stretch out. The cast had recently come off, but his leg still felt weak.

"You okay?"

"Arm's a little tired."

"You going to let me take over?" She smiled as she watched him.

It was the same question she asked each time she noticed his fatigue, and he loved her for it. However, he wasn't handing the oars over. Not today. "I'm good." He started rowing again, ignoring the residual ache.

If it was anything like his other injuries, it'd probably always linger, having more good days than bad.

His mind wondered toward the picnic area where he planned to propose. Mrs. Williams was bringing the food and the boys. Dwight and Nina would attend the mini celebration as well.

Unfortunately, the only thing he hadn't prepared for was his speech. The picnic area was set up just like last time, with the checkered blanket and picnic basket. He had the same playlist ready and waiting on his cell phone.

Sure, it was the exact same idea from their first date, but he hoped he would gain more points than lose any.

Of course, the rose gold engagement ring with the round diamond was supposed to seal the deal. He'd scoured over hundreds of wedding rings online, hoping to find the right one.

The rose setting was his top choice and nothing beat it, so he stopped looking. He wasn't sure if it was the twisted band design that held smaller diamonds, or the rose-colored gold.

Whatever it was, he hoped Delaney would agree it was perfect.

"I'm so glad summer is beginning to fade away."

"Can't tell by the temperature today."

Delaney chuckled. "That's Virginia for you. Sixty-five degrees yesterday and eighty today."

"At least today isn't too humid."

"Amen." She grinned at him.

Just as he thought, the fall foliage added another layer of charm to the picnic area. Golds, oranges, and burnt reds glowed in the sun's light.

Luke got out of the boat, securing it before helping Delaney out. He focused on the task at hand, trying to prevent nerves from edging him into panic mode.

His mind kicked into overdrive, wondering about her reaction to the ring box burning a hole through his jeans. Maybe he'd just beg for her hand in marriage in the boat.

Keep calm, Robinson. Be smooth, not desperate.

But he *was* desperate. He knew he'd never find another woman like Delaney. Didn't even want to try. She was it for him. They'd have to do a reverse of their first date.

The picnic basket was merely for show, since Mrs. Williams was coming with a spread to feed the entire family.

"Dance with me?"

She nodded, moving into his arms with practiced ease. They swayed under the sunlight as strands of country songs filled the air. Delaney laid her head against his chest and his heart swelled.

"This is probably my favorite thing to do with you, Luke."

"Go on a picnic?"

"Dance."

He pulled away and stared into her beautiful brown eyes. "Will you dance with me for the next fifty years, Delaney Jane Jones?"

She blinked. "Wait, what?"

He let go of her hand and took the black box out of his pocket. Inhaling, then exhaling, he slowly lowered himself on his right leg.

It wasn't a hundred percent, but that was okay. He didn't need it to be in order to dance with the love of his life. Nor kneel and ask her to do him the greatest honor.

"Delaney Jane Jones, would you do me the honor of being my wife? Of loving me and dancing with me for the next fifty plus years?"

"Oh, Luke." Tears filled her eyes and her hand shook as she held it out.

"I need to hear the words, darlin'."

"Yes, I'll marry you."

Pure unadulterated joy filled his heart. He scooped her up and twirled her around, loving the sound of her heartfelt laughter.

"Thank goodness," he whispered.

"Did you have any doubt?"

"Maybe."

"I may have been hesitant in the beginning," she said, staring into his eyes. "But when you find love, you have to grab hold of it and never let go. You're stuck with me, Luke Robinson."

"Hallelujah," he said with a grin.

Philip watched as Mr. Luke twirled his mom around. They laughed as some country dude sang about stars. Seemed kind of silly to him, but his Mom tilted her head back, laughing, a whole big smile covering her face.

Guess she liked this kind of music.

He looked around and noticed Pres stuffing his face with food. His eyes practically popped out of his head when Grandma laid all the food out. Figures, he'd think of his stomach first.

Everyone looked like they were having a good time. It was just as it should be. It felt like a real family, the kind he saw on TV. This was the life.

Thank You, God, for bringing Mr. Luke to our family. Thanks for answering my prayer.

When he first prayed to God, he didn't know who the answer to his prayer would be, but knew God would answer it. Grandma said God always answered your prayer, even when it didn't look like it, and today was proof.

His Mom was going to marry Mr. Luke.

He and Pres would have a father again. His mom would stop being sad, and his grandmother could stop worrying about everyone. He knew Mr. Luke would retire from the Army, which made his mom really happy, though he had no clue what a medical retirement was.

Whatever it was, it seemed to make both Mr. Luke and his mom happy. He didn't care. Just happy that his family was whole once more.

Before his mom met Mr. Luke, he used to pray for a dad. The first time he did it, he thought he'd hurl. Pres thought it was the gummy worms, and he was too ashamed to say otherwise.

His real dad had been a good one, but he was fading from his memory, even though he slept with his picture under his pillow to keep the memories close.

After that, he'd asked God to make sure his real dad was okay that his mom got married again.

Philip was pretty sure his dad wanted someone watching over them. Uncle D couldn't do it because his family kept growing. First there was Kandi, then Gabe and Abby.

Now Aunt Nina was going to have another baby. Nope, Uncle D couldn't do the job anymore.

That was just fine. Now they had Mr. Luke. He frowned, feeling his forehead scrunch up all weird like. Hopefully the lines wouldn't get stuck like they were in his grandmother's forehead. Then again, she was kind of old.

He sighed. *What was I thinking about?* Oh yeah, he was thinking about what to call Mr. Luke. Would he let him and Pres call him Dad? He watched as his mom stopped dancing and walked over to his grandmother. Maybe now he could ask.

Philip ran over to him before Preston appeared out of nowhere and could take over the conversation. His brother never paused long enough for anyone else to talk. He loved the guy, but he really needed to shut up.

"Hey, Mr. Luke."

"Hey, bud." Mr. Luke stooped over. "Thanks for keeping my secret."

Philip grinned. "I don't talk as much as some people."

Mr. Luke laughed. "I know you don't. But you have a lot to say, huh?"

"I do." He bit his lip, "Mr. Luke?"

"Yes, Philip?"

"Could I call you something else? I mean, besides Mr. Luke?" He stopped, suddenly wondering if he sounded as silly as he did in his head.

"What do you want to call me, bud?"

He inhaled, gathering courage. "I thought Dad sounded like a good idea."

Mr. Luke's face got a huge grin on it. Holes appeared in his cheeks. "Dad sounds like a perfect idea, Philip."

His face heated up but he forged on. "And can you maybe call me son?" He wiped his hands on his jeans, wondering why they felt sweaty.

"I'd love to call you son. Scout's honor?"

"Nah, how about a fist bump?"

"Fist bump it is."

They bumped fists, then Mr. Luke – no – Dad, pulled him up into his arms and hugged him.

"Love you, son."

"Love you too, Dad."

Note from the Author

Dear Readers,

I pray you enjoyed Delaney and Luke's story. Finding Love holds a special place in my heart and might be one of my favorite stories. Could you help spread the word? A review goes a long way to help authors, whether good or bad. If you'd take a moment to leave an honest review, I'd really appreciate it.

Blessings,
Toni Shiloh

Other Books by Toni

Buying Love
It's a wonderful novel, sweet, funny, and enjoyable. Loved the characters, too, they're relatable, realistic, flawed, and honest. Each of the main ones had their own personal issues to work through. The plot was a fun play on finding a mate. Recommend to anyone looking for a great, clean, and faithfilled book.

A Spring of Weddings
Was excited to read this story and not disappointed. This is well-written with well-developed characters who the author endears to her readers. This easy to read story is fresh and captivating with an engaging style. Toni writes with grace and faith. Trust me this story will grab your attention, then stick with you long after the end. It's hard to put down until the end.

Do you have a book you are looking to have published?

Celebrate Lit Publishing is currently accepting manuscripts for consideration.

For more information, visit www.celebratelitpublishing.com

Contact the Author

Toni Shiloh is a wife, mom, and Christian fiction writer. She is a member of the American Christian Fiction Writers (ACFW), an Air Force veteran, and a member of the body of Christ.
She spends her days hanging out with her husband and their two boys. She likes to volunteer at her children's school. When she's not writing, she's reading. An avid reader of Christian fiction, she writes reviews on her blog and enjoys helping other authors find readers.

Amazon : https://www.amazon.com/Toni-Shiloh/e/B00UITVEDA

Facebook : www.facebook.com/authortonishiloh

Website : tonishiloh.weebly.com/

Google+ : https://plus.google.com/u/0/116452363653059921235/posts

LinkedIn : https://www.linkedin.com/in/tonishiloh

Blogs : Personal , Soulfully Romantic ~ http://tonishiloh.weebly.com/blog

HeartWings ~ http://www.heartwingsblog.com

Made in the USA
Coppell, TX
25 May 2021